Also by Maureen Bartone

Life In The Gumball Machine – Vinnie A

Tilly's Top-Secret Trapdoor
National Indie Excellence Awards® FINALIST

Illustrations by MikeMotz.com

Twin Cities, MN / Maureen Bartone — First Edition

ISBN-13: 978-0692694862

ISBN-10: 0692694862

Printed in the United States of America

Contact Maureen Bartone at: Maureen@MaureenBartoneAuthor.com

Subjects include: time travel, time travel fiction, time travel books, science fiction, humorous fiction, family relationships, friendship, sword & sorcery, social skills & school life, growing up & facts of life, science fiction & scary stories, fantasy & magic, chapter books, middle grade books, kids' reading, reading, literature & fiction, humorous, gumball machine

Life In The Gumball Machine

* * *

Maureen Bartone

*For my daughters,
Danielle and Brittani,
I love you!*

Life In The
Gumball Machine

1 Daisy

DAISY WAS MAD. Her two best friends, Patrick and Michael, left to play football with the guys. That was one sport she did *not* like to play. She was shorter than the other fourth graders in their class, and she hated being tackled.

It hurt!

She usually played all the other cool sports with the boys, like baseball, basketball, and soccer—but, not football.

Daisy would be sure to give them a piece of her mind when they returned from their fun and games. They didn't even ask her if she wanted to play. Oh, well. Who was she kidding? Why would they ask her to play football when they already knew the answer? Still, she was mad.

Some of the girls at school called Daisy a tomboy because she hung out with boys.

What is a tomboy, anyway?

One of the boys at school said a tomboy is a girl who has boy-short hair, wears boy clothes, climbs trees, and plays with worms. Then he said, "It's a girl who looks and acts like a boy—duh!"

I am *not* a tomboy, she told herself. She certainly didn't think she *looked* like a boy. She didn't have boy-short hair or wear boy clothes. What are boy clothes, anyway? She wore dresses—sometimes.

According to her grandma, Daisy's eyes were as blue as the sky. Daisy's mom said that her shoulder-length, wavy blond hair was very pretty when she wore it down. But Daisy didn't like to wear it down. She usually wore her hair in a ponytail or pigtails so it wouldn't get in the way while she played.

Does that make me a tomboy? No. Wearing my hair in a ponytail does not make me a tomboy. And worms? No way! Gross!

Not only did Daisy hate being called a tomboy, she often complained to her mom that she was shorter than almost everyone in her class. Her mom kept promising her that she would have a "growth spurt," but she wondered when that would happen.

Her friends, Patrick and Michael, were tall for fourth graders. Michael, age ten, was one of the smartest and funniest kids in their class, and he knew how to crack a joke without hurting anyone's feelings. Most of the kids liked him a lot. His warm, brown eyes twinkled when he smiled, and his light brown, spiked hair was usually hidden under a baseball cap worn backward. He was starting to get muscles from all the sports he played, too. His pants were always baggy and his shirts were often un-tucked and much too big for him, but still, the girls in their class thought he was cute. Michael didn't like that. He thought girls were annoying. Daisy never thought of him as cute. She never paid attention to stuff like that.

Daisy's other friend, Patrick, was one of the oldest kids in their class. At age eleven, not only was he taller than both Daisy and Michael, he was skinnier, too. His sandy blond hair was so straight, it moved when his head moved—which was all the time. He wore braces on his teeth and had freckles that sprinkled across his nose and cheeks. The twinkle in his eyes was hard to see because of his large glasses, which were always sliding down his nose. He was supposed to wear them all the time, but he often left them at home, because they were too big. He hated them, but his mom bought the larger size so he could grow into them. She said it would save lots of money. Whenever he forgot them, he had to scrunch his face and eyes so he could see. Sometimes, he would bang his shin on a chair or a table. Daisy and Michael would laugh whenever he did that because he always said "ooh-owie" instead of just "owe."

Patrick was funny, but he never *meant* to be funny. He was a little clumsy, even when he remembered to wear his glasses, and often tripped over his own feet. He called it bad luck. Sometimes, he would step into icky things or spill food on his shirt. This would upset him because he liked being neat. His shirts were always clean and tucked into his pants. Whenever he spilled something on his shirt or stepped into mud or other nasty things, Daisy and Michael couldn't help but chuckle. They could always count on a good laugh whenever they were with Patrick. Even though Patrick tried hard to look nice, he wasn't as popular with the girls, and for this, he was extremely happy. Girls scared him!

The thing Daisy liked most about the boys was that they always made her laugh. The three of them laughed all the time. The boys liked having Daisy for a friend, too. They thought it was cool that she liked playing all the games they liked to play. They never thought about her being a girl, except when she refused to play football. They wondered why it was such a big deal to her. They would tell her she was acting like a big baby, and being tackled didn't hurt that much. They wished she would try it again, and often begged her to join them in a game, just to see if she would change her mind, but she always refused.

"One day," Patrick told her, "we'll get you to play a game of football with us."

"Not on your life," was how she always responded.

Daisy loved playing with Michael and Patrick and hanging out with them, but she also liked–what her older brother, Joe, called–"girlie" things. She dreamed of a friend who would play jump-rope with her, have dress-up parties, make beaded jewelry, wear lipstick and pretty flowered dresses, and whisper about some of the cute boys in school. She wished for this every day. She could never confess this to Michael and Patrick, or anyone for that matter, and she couldn't do any of that "girlie" stuff unless she did it by herself, and there is no fun in that. If only she had a "girl" friend.

Unfortunately, wishing was all Daisy could do. There were no girls in her neighborhood. All the girls from school lived too far from her house. Sure, they hung out in school, but that wasn't enough. After all, you have to go to class, and listen, and sit up straight, and be quiet. Plus, most of the girls in school thought Daisy was a tomboy. They were nice to her, and she knew they were just joking about the tomboy thing, but she had no true best girlfriend. She had no one she could share her love of the "girlie" things.

So, there she was, sitting on her front porch, with nothing to do. She heard a noise and turned her head in time to see her mother at the screen door carrying two glasses of lemonade. Daisy jumped up to help her open the door.

"Thanks," said her mom, as she handed Daisy one of the cold glasses.

They sat down on the top step of the front porch, drinking their lemonade in silence. It was a warm day, and Daisy thought the cool drink tasted delicious. It was sweet and tart and made her cheeks pucker, and her left eye squint shut after each sip. It was nice to sit quietly with her mom and listen to the gentle sounds of summer–the chirping birds, the buzzing bugs, and the rustling of the leaves stirred by a slight breeze. She enjoyed these quiet times.

Daisy's mom was tall and thin, with shoulder-length curly blond hair and blue eyes. Daisy's dad always said that Daisy got her hair and eye color from her mom. Daisy liked that. Her mom was pretty, and she hoped that one day she would look just like her.

Her mom always knew when Daisy was feeling lonely and she knew how to cheer her up, too. She could see that Daisy was bothered by something. She took a sip of the lemonade and said, "Guess what, Daisy?"

Daisy looked up at her mom for an answer.

Pointing off to the left, her mom said, "There's a new family moving in across the street, at the Donaldson's old house. Do you see the moving truck? I saw a man taking down the 'sold' sign just this morning. And right after that, the movers started unloading their furniture."

Daisy shrugged and nodded.

Her mom continued. "Mrs. Baker told me the new neighbors have a daughter, named Violet. She's ten years old, just like you. Isn't that great?"

Daisy's heart skipped a beat as she turned to her mom. "Really? That's so awesome! I can't wait to meet her! Do you think she's over there yet? Will you come with me to meet her? I'll be too scared."

Daisy stopped chattering. "Wait a minute. I'm not ten years old yet," she said, rolling her eyes.

"Well, your birthday is tomorrow, so you're *almost* ten."

"Yay! Finally! I've been waiting *forever* to be ten, like Michael. Patrick keeps calling me a wimp because I'm only nine and he's a big-shot eleven-year-old. He thinks he's *so* cool and smart. They've been teasing me for months. I'm catching up to them! Yes!"

Daisy's mom smiled. "Don't rush it, Daisy. Life goes by fast enough. Enjoy being a kid while you can."

"Whatever, Mom."

"Whatever, Daisy," said her mom, smiling. "Did the boys say they were coming to your party?"

"Yes, they both can come."

"Good. Hey—I have an idea. What do you think about asking Violet to your party? It would be a great way for her to get to know you and the kids from school and the neighborhood. You have no idea how hard it is to start a new school. No one knows you and you have no friends. It's *pretty* scary."

"Hey, that's a great idea! You're pretty smart—for a mom."

They nudged each other's shoulders and laughed. Daisy enjoyed the times she spent talking to her mom. She always knew how to cheer her up.

Of course, her dad was pretty awesome, too. He was funny, smart, and she often asked him for help with her homework. Still, he didn't understand her like her mom did. It must be a girl-thing.

Her big brother, Joe, was a *completely* different story. He teased her and always tried to make her mad. Daisy was pretty sure he *enjoyed* being awful to her. He was thirteen years old, with dark brown hair, like their dad. But, unlike their dad, Joe was mean, obnoxious, and annoying to her, every day of her life. Plus, he was a big kid, much taller than Daisy, and pretty beefy, too. She didn't like to mess with him too much. He was very strong and had no mercy.

Daisy's younger brother, Sammie, was eight years old. He was alright—for a little kid. He was shorter than Daisy, but was quickly catching up to her. He had blond hair and blue eyes, too. They got their looks from their mom. Both of her brothers were usually so annoying that she sometimes wished she were an only child.

Daisy and her mom continued sitting quietly on the porch drinking their lemonade. She could smell her mom's flowers in the nearby pots. Their house sat on a quiet street, with few cars ever driving by. Daisy had to remember to be careful crossing, though, because, according to her dad, "You never know when someone driving too fast might race up the street."

Daisy turned to her mom. "What kind of a name is Violet, anyway?"

"Violet is a beautiful purple flower, just like those," her mother said, pointing to some flowers on a bush near the steps.

"Oh, that's a nice name," Daisy said.

She was excited that—finally— a girl was moving into the neighborhood. She could hardly wait to meet her. She hoped she was nice and that they'd become best friends. It would be awesome if Violet could come to her birthday party tomorrow. Her stomach fluttered at the thought.

2 Violet

VIOLET WAS A PRETTY GIRL who had long, dark
the middle of her back. She often pulled it back into a braid, with a purple
bow placed on the end. Purple was her favorite color, "Like the violet
flower," her mother always said. Violet–the girl–not the flower–had large
brown eyes with long lashes and beautiful brown skin.

She liked her new house. As she looked out her upstairs bedroom
window, Violet wondered about the blond-haired girl sitting on the porch
across the street. She also wondered if the girl was her age and whether
they'd become friends. She hoped they would. I'll bet she's nice, she
thought, as she imagined them playing together.

Violet hadn't noticed any other kids of her culture in the neighborhood
when she and her parents first drove into town. That scared her a little bit.
When they went into a store near their new house this morning, a woman
stared at them. That made Violet's stomach feel funny.

"Mom, why did that lady stare at us?"

"She was just 'noticing' us because we're new to the neighborhood,"
said her mom. "That's all. Try not to let it bother you, sweetie."

But it *did* bother her. She didn't know why, but it did. She did *not* like
the nervous feeling in her stomach. People never stared at them in their
old neighborhood, so this was a new experience for her. She didn't like it.
Her parents promised her that everything would be fine. She hoped they
were right.

Despite being a little scared, Violet did like her new house. It was much
bigger than their townhouse back in Chicago. However, she did miss her
friends from her old school and the old neighborhood.

"Daddy has a big new job, and things will be much better for us now,"
her mom explained.

Violet hoped she was right. Except for the people in the store, she had
a good feeling about this place.

****

LATER THAT DAY, Daisy kneeled on the couch in her living room,
looking out the front window. She wanted to go across the street and

duce herself to the new girl, but she was a little nervous. She wondered what Violet looked like, and whether she was nice. She quickly decided that it didn't really matter what she looked like. She just hoped she was nice and would want to play with her.

Daisy saw movement from the corner of her eye. A girl who looked her age was walking around toward the front of the Donaldson's old house. The butterflies in Daisy's stomach returned.

I wonder if that's Violet.

At that moment, Patrick and Michael walked in from the kitchen. Daisy's mom had let them in through the back door.

"What are you doing, Daisy?" asked Michael, as they jumped on the couch to join her. Daisy nearly fell to the floor.

"Hey, stop! I told you—my mom doesn't want any jumping on the couch!" Daisy yelled.

"Okay, okay. S-o-r-r-y! We forgot," Patrick chuckled.

The two boys high-fived each other behind Daisy's back. They loved making her mad.

Returning to look out the window, Daisy told them she was checking out her new neighbor.

"I'm going over there to invite her to my birthday party."

Just then, Daisy's big brother, Joe, walked into the room. Even though he was only a few years older, he was much bigger and loved to act mean and tough. He was always trying to bully them. Patrick and Michael were afraid of him. Daisy couldn't stand him.

"What are you *doofs* looking at?" Joe shouted, startling the three children.

Daisy snapped back at him. "We're looking at our new neighbor, if it's any of your business."

"Oh, yeah, I saw her already," Joe sneered.

Daisy ignored his mean tone.

"I was thinking about going over there and inviting her to my party," she said.

Joe laughed. "You'd be crazy to invite *her* to your party. What will all your other friends think? I bet they won't even show up if they find out *she's* coming," he said laughing.

Even though he knew it wasn't true, Joe wanted Daisy to believe it was. He loved to trick her, and she was so easy to tease. He laughed and strolled back to the kitchen.

Daisy felt as if Joe had punched her in the stomach. She looked at her two friends. They stared back at her, shaking their heads. They couldn't believe how mean Joe could be.

"Do you think that's true? Do you think no one else would come to my party if I invited her? That's not very nice, is it?" asked Daisy.

"I don't know. Maybe Joe's right," Patrick said, shaking his head.

"Yeah, but that's really mean," Daisy said. "My friends would never be like that. How about you two? Would you guys come if I invited her?"

Both boys nodded. "Yep. We'd come for sure," said Michael. "You should never treat someone mean like that. My mom taught me that a long time ago. I can't believe Joe hasn't learned that yet."

Patrick and Daisy nodded.

"But I don't know, Daisy," Michael said, "I'm not sure what your friends might do. I just know what *I'd* do."

From across the hall, they heard Joe say, "Do whatever you want, but I know you'd love to have a lot of people and lots of presents at your party." He smiled as he walked upstairs. He loved to confuse his little sister.

Daisy rubbed her forehead and frowned. She didn't know what to think or do. She decided not to go across the street and introduce herself–not yet. She had to think. Something didn't feel right. This was wrong, yet her brother seemed to know what he was talking about. He is older, thought Daisy. She also secretly hoped for lots of presents.

Wrong, wrong. It all feels wrong!

"Come on," Patrick said, "let's go out back and play catch."

They got up and started toward the kitchen. Daisy took one last look out the window at the new girl. She looked so lonely.

3 Daisy's New Bike

THE NEXT MORNING, Daisy slowly opened her eyes. She could hear the robins tweeting outside her bedroom window. She squirmed around for a few minutes and then sat up. Today was her birthday!

Yay!

Finally! Ten years old, just like the guys—and just like Violet. Her heart sank and her excitement vanished. She decided not to think about Violet—not yet, anyway. It's my birthday, she told herself, and I'm going to enjoy it.

She put on her robe, ran downstairs and immediately searched for a special present. When she looked in the living room, her face lit up. There, in the middle of the room, sat a *huge* box. It was colorfully decorated with paper, ribbons, and bows. A banner taped to the side it read:

HAPPY BIRTHDAY, DAISY!

She laughed as she ran to it. Her dad had been standing in the hall where Daisy couldn't see him. He wanted to see her face when she first saw the present. He was almost as excited to see her expression, as she was to open the present.

"Go ahead, open it," he said, as he came into the living room.

Her dad was tall and thin with short, brown hair. He had a warm smile. She looked up at him and saw the twinkle of excitement in his brown eyes. She sure did love him.

Daisy knew what was inside. She ripped off the paper and saw a plain box underneath.

"Help me, Dad!"

She pulled and yanked at the edges of the cardboard.

"Here," said her dad, "let me show you how easy it is."

As he lifted the box straight up, Daisy started to giggle. In front of her, she saw a beautiful pink bicycle. It had a flowered basket on the front and shiny paper streamers coming out of the handlebars. The seat was pink and sparkly and—oh boy—it was big. She had hoped it wasn't too big. It didn't matter. She *loved* it!

She had wanted it ever since she and her dad saw it in the department store at the mall. It had been on display near the store's entrance, and she had asked him to wait while she watched another girl sit on it. She had laughed when she thought how much Patrick and Michael would *hate* the pink color. After the other girl left, she walked up to it and touched the handlebars. She turned to her dad and told him how much she loved it, and how much she wanted it.

"Oh please, Dad, can we get it? It's the most beautiful bike I've ever seen."

Her dad told her they couldn't get the bike that day because it was too expensive, and he couldn't afford it.

"Maybe someday," he told her.

Someday means never.

Now, that very bike was in her living room. She still couldn't believe it.

Giving him a big bear hug, she said, "Oh Dad. I love it! Thank you, thank you, thank you! I *knew* you'd get it for me."

He smiled. "How did you *know* I'd get it? I told you I wouldn't buy it for you because it was too expensive."

"Oh come on, Dad. I knew you were joking."

She turned back to admire her beautiful bike. She couldn't wait to ride it.

"Can I take it outside and ride it? Now? P-l-e-a-s-e? Can I, Dad?"

"Well, first you have to get dressed, sweetheart. You can't ride your bike outside in your pajamas. What would the neighbors think?" He rubbed the top of her head.

Daisy laughed. "Oh, right. Whoops!"

"After you change, you can take it for a spin, but remember to wear your helmet, and be careful."

Daisy ran to the stairs. "Don't worry Dad, I will!" She climbed a few stairs and stopped. Turning, she shouted, "Thanks again, Dad! You're the best!"

Oh boy. Wait until Patrick and Michael see what I got for my birthday, she thought. This will make their bikes look like junk. She chuckled to herself as she quickly changed into a pair of shorts, a red t-shirt, and her tennis shoes. She brushed her hair and ran back downstairs.

"This is *so* cool, Dad. I can't wait to show all the kids at my party."

"That's a great idea," her dad said, as he started for the kitchen. "Oh, by the way, have you decided whether you'll invite our new neighbor to the party? Your mother said you were thinking about it."

Daisy looked at the floor. "I was thinking about it, but I haven't met her yet."

Her dad stopped and looked at her.

"Well, what are you waiting for? Go over there and introduce yourself. Welcome her to the neighborhood."

Daisy frowned.

"What's wrong?"

"I'm afraid," she said.

"What are you afraid of?"

She didn't want to tell him what her rotten brother Joe said. If she did, then Joe would get in trouble, and if Joe got in trouble, he'd come looking for her. She did *not* want that because it usually meant a hard pound in her arm.

No thanks.

She especially didn't want to admit to her dad that she was actually afraid she'd have fewer friends and presents if she invited Violet. She knew that was wrong, but yet, she couldn't help thinking about it, and she was afraid it might be true. Maybe she'd lose all of her other friends.

I wouldn't lose Patrick or Michael. They already told me that.

What kind of friends would the rest of them be if they acted like that? Does she even *want* friends like that? Are presents more important than a person's feelings? She knew the answer, and it made her ashamed. She was so confused.

Her dad interrupted her thoughts. "Come on, Daisy. Tell me what's bothering you."

"Oh, I don't know," she said. "Maybe she won't want to come to my party, Dad."

"Don't be silly. Go over there. You'll never know until you ask her."

"Okay," she whispered.

Just then, Patrick and Michael knocked on the door. Daisy's dad went to answer it.

"Hello there, boys. Come on in."

"Happy birthday Dais'," Patrick said.

"Yes, happy birthday," Michael said. "So—you're finally ten. It's about time." He folded his arms and smiled.

"Thanks," Daisy said. "Hey! Look what I got!" She pointed to her new bike.

The three of them ran up to it.

"Whoa, dude!" shouted Michael.

"Cool!" Patrick said, touching the smooth handlebars.

"Let's take it for a spin. Do you guys have your bikes with you?" asked Daisy.

Michael rolled his eyes. "No, we walked."

They laughed as they pushed Daisy's new bike out the back door and carried it down the steps. The three of them put on their helmets, mounted their bikes, and started down the driveway laughing and joking, as usual. They turned right and headed up the street toward the playground. Daisy slowed down and glanced at Violet's house. She didn't see her new neighbor, so she pumped her pedals and picked up speed.

"Wait up you guys!"

***

FROM HER BEDROOM WINDOW, Violet heard voices and laughter coming from outside. She peered around the curtain at the three kids and watched them disappear up the street. She'd never felt so lonely. She wished she were riding with them, wherever they were going.

4 The Gumball Machine

SIDE-BY-SIDE, DAISY, MICHAEL, AND PATRICK rode down the street. Michael suggested they take a shortcut down an alley so they could get to the playground faster. He hooked a left, and the other two followed him, talking and laughing as they pedaled as fast as they could, trying to race each other. Michael was in the lead when Daisy and Patrick noticed him slow down. Michael stopped and they caught up with him.

"What's up?" Daisy asked.

"Look over there!" Michael whispered. He got off his bike and put the kickstand down. The other two did the same.

"What are you looking at?" Patrick asked.

"Shh. It's a little bunny. I saw it run back here," Michael said.

He walked around an old shed standing next to a rundown garage. Near the shed and garage, was a short sidewalk leading up to a wooden fence with chipped, brown paint. Beyond the fence, Daisy could see two piles of trash, and a couple of old tires. Just past the piles of trash sat an old, worn-down house. It too had chipped, brown paint, and most of its windows were broken. Daisy thought the house looked a little haunted. There was no one around and it was quiet and spooky.

"I don't think we should be here," she said. "This doesn't look too safe, and that house is kind of scary. Come on. Forget the little bunny. You'll never catch it anyway. Let's go."

"No," Michael whined. "He's trapped back here. There is no *way* he can escape. I think we should try to capture him. He could be our little pet."

"Michael, we don't need a pet. We all have dogs. And good luck trying to catch a bunny. Do you know how fast they are? It would be a million years before we caught him. Come on, let's go," she said.

Now, Patrick was back there with Michael trying to figure out a way to catch the bunny.

"Look inside the shed and see if you can find anything we can use to trap him," Patrick said to Daisy.

Daisy moaned. She didn't want to mess with a bunny. She wanted to ride her new bike. She kept her mouth shut and reached for the door handle to the old shed. It was heavy, but she pulled and pulled until she finally got it to move.

"Shh! Daisy, keep it down. You're scaring him," Michael whispered.

Daisy ignored him and peered into the shed. It was dark and dirty and smelled like dust. Tiny slivers of sunlight peeked through the wooden walls, but still, it was hard to see where she was going. She tiptoed inside and was two feet into the shed when the door slammed shut. She screamed, startling the boys, who came running up to the closed shed door. Together they struggled to open it.

Patrick peeked inside. "Are you alright Daisy?"

"Yes, but that really scared me. Prop it open with a rock or something, so we aren't trapped in here. I think I found something cool."

Patrick propped the door with a large brick he found lying outside the shed.

"Is it something to put the bunny in?" Michael asked.

"No. Forget that bunny," she said.

"What did you find Daisy?" asked Patrick, coming to stand next to her.

Pointing, Daisy said, "Look. It's an old gumball machine. It's a big one, too!"

The gumball machine was almost as tall as she was, and it was filled to the top with colorful gumballs. It was also filthy. Daisy wiped the dust away from the large globe and smeared it onto her shorts. Moving closer, the three of them peered in to admire what looked like a thousand gumballs.

Michael smiled. "Look at all of those gumballs! They're huge!"

Daisy looked at the money slot to see the price for one gumball. "Does anyone have a nickel?" she asked, without looking up.

"Are you sure you want a gumball that looks like it's a hundred years old? You might break a tooth," Patrick said, reaching into his pocket and handing her a nickel.

"Yeah, Daisy. What's the big deal, anyway?" asked Michael. "Come on. The bunny's going to get away."

"Well, the gumballs *might* still be good," Daisy said. "Besides, I've never seen a gumball machine this big before and I want to watch a gumball come swirling down this tunnel." She pointed to the spiral slide that led to the opening at the bottom. "This is a long tunnel, too, so the ride will be even cooler to watch."

The two boys rolled their eyes and watched as she placed the coin into the slot and turned the crank. She heard the gumball start rolling before she actually saw it. And then—there it was.

Daisy smiled. "Look! A red one! Here it comes!"

They bent forward and watched as the red gumball rolled around and down the spiral track until it landed at the bottom of the machine, near Daisy's ankles. She crouched down and, reaching in, took the red gumball out of the slot. She placed it near her mouth and the boys groaned as they put their hands up to stop her.

Patrick banged his fist on the bowl of gumballs. "Don't eat that Daisy! You'll get sick!"

Just then, they heard a noise—like a bump—behind the gumball machine.

"It's the bunny!" whispered Michael.

As he peered around the machine, they heard another bump. This time, it was louder and they jumped back.

"No bunny makes a sound like *that*," said Daisy.

"What the heck *was* that?" Patrick asked, grabbing Michael's sleeve.

"I don't know," said Daisy.

She placed her hands on top of the gumball machine to look behind it. As she touched it, the whole thing rumbled and an orange gumball started rolling down the track. They watched as it rolled down its twirling course. When the orange gumball landed at the bottom, Daisy looked at the two boys and hesitated, before reaching in to remove it. As she touched the slot, she immediately noticed a funny feeling in her hands and arms.

"Whoa! What was that?" she said, yanking back her hand.

Patrick rubbed his hands. "What? What do you mean?"

"I don't know. I just felt something *weird*," Daisy said. "Like a vibration. You know—like a buzzing. Buzz-z-z." She rubbed her hands on the sides of her legs.

"Maybe we should get out of here," Patrick said, looking toward the door.

Michael ignored Patrick and looked at Daisy. "A vibration? Are you sure?"

"Yeah, I'm sure. Go ahead. Try it. It's weird."

"Okay," said Michael. "Give me another nickel."

Patrick checked his pockets. "I'm out."

"Wow, *you're* rich," said Michael.

He checked his own pockets and took out a bunch of change. He grabbed a nickel and inserted it. He too immediately noticed a strange vibration in his hands and arms.

Buzz-z-z.

"Hey. That's kind of cool," he said, giggling.

They watched as a large yellow gumball rolled through the tunnel and down into the slot. Michael bent down and removed his yellow gumball.

"Let me try," said Patrick.

His hand shook a little as he took a nickel from Michael's hand and inserted it into the coin slot. As he slowly turned the crank, he felt a tickling sensation go up his right arm, across the back of his shoulders, and down his left arm. It continued to travel all the way down his left leg to his toes. As he finished turning the crank, he let out a big hiccup.

"H-i-c-c-u-p!"

A green gumball rolled through the tunnel toward the opening at the bottom.

"Oh! That is *so* weird!"

"Let's do it again!" said Daisy, giggling.

"Is this thing plugged in or something?" asked Michael, looking around to the back of the machine.

They looked around and behind it, but could see no electrical cord.

"It's not plugged in. Isn't that weird? How could it be making any noise or rumble like that without electricity?" Michael asked.

Daisy took the green gumball out of the slot and handed it to Patrick. So far, none of them had been brave enough to put one into their mouth. She then placed Michael's last nickel into the coin slot and turned the crank. This time, as she turned it, she too hiccupped and started to wobble back and forth. Her whole body shook and shuddered.

"Whoa—whoa!"

The vibration was stronger than before and it rushed through her entire body, causing her to stiffen like a board. As another red gumball came swirling down the tunnel, Daisy's body started to jerk. The boys looked at each other and then back at Daisy.

She tried to shake off the strange feeling as she reached down to grab the gumball, but her body started rolling and wobbling in a circle. She looked to the boys for help. As she touched the red gumball, she felt her arm being pulled and sucked into the slot, bringing her down to her knees.

Daisy looked up at the boys. "Ahh! You guys–*help*!"

Michael and Patrick reached for her, but when they touched her arms, they too started hiccupping and wobbling back and forth. Their bodies stiffened as the vibration coming from Daisy's body jumped to Patrick and then to Michael.

The boys were jerked to the floor, bumping into each other and banging into Daisy. They felt their bodies curl forward. They tried hard to straighten out, but the pull was too strong.

"We're shrinking!" Daisy screamed.

"Ahh! Help!" Patrick yelled.

"Help! Somebody! Help!" Michael shouted.

Their bodies jerked, shrinking smaller and smaller until they were as tiny as the gumballs. A sucking force–like a strong wind–roared and pulled them to the opening at the bottom of the gumball machine. No matter how hard they tried, they couldn't fight it as it pulled them through the slot, sucking them into the swirling tunnel and up toward the top of the gumball machine.

5 Spinning

INSIDE THE SWIRLING TUNNEL, Daisy, Patrick, and Michael could only scream as they were sucked up and around in a spinning motion. Round and round they went, getting dizzier and dizzier. Daisy was first. Patrick was behind her, and Michael was behind Patrick. Their arms flew wildly above their heads, as the sucking force twisted and pulled them up, up, up. A loud roar blasted in their ears as they swirled and twirled and spun up the tunnel.

"Daisy! What's Going On?" Patrick shouted.

"I don't know!" she cried.

"I'm going to lose my glasses!" he screamed. "Ahh! I'm *so* dizzy! Mom! Dad! Somebody help us!"

From far below her, Daisy heard Michael scream. "Ahh! Ahh! Ahh!"

She worried that they were too far up into the machine for anyone to hear them. The temperature dropped, and Daisy felt the air getting colder and colder. The cold air bit her skin and froze her fingers and feet.

The trip up the spiral tunnel lasted only a short while, but to Daisy, it seemed like an eternity. As they approached the top, they were sucked through the opening and thrown up into the gumball machine. Once inside, they flew through the air until they crashed into the top of the gumball machine's clear bowl.

Crash! Bang! Boom!

Daisy's back slammed hard into the top of the bowl. "Owe!"

For a split second, it felt like she was floating as she grabbed her head and looked down.

It's like a dream!

Everything was blurry, but still, it was a beautiful, colorful, blur. She felt herself drop and looked over at Michael and Patrick, their bodies flopping through the sky. They fell fast, crashing down on top of each other.

"Ugh!"

Daisy and Michael fell on top of Patrick and everyone groaned as they pushed away from each other and sat up. Daisy rubbed her aching head as she looked to see if Patrick and Michael were okay.

Michael whined, rubbing his hands and arms. "You guys—I'm *so* c-c-o-l-d!"

Patrick put his hands out in front of him and then up to his cheeks. "I c-c-can't s-s-see! I c-c-can't s-s-see!"

"Your g-g-glasses fell off, Patrick. D-d-don't w-w-worry. We'll f-f-find them," said Michael.

"Oh. G-g-good. I th-th-thought my eyes were f-f-frozen shut."

They crawled around looking for his glasses. Patrick finally found them himself and put them on. The lenses were a little frosty around the edges, but he was happy to be able to see again.

"You g-g-guys have f-f-frost all over you," Daisy said, shaking and shivering.

She looked at the boys and then down at herself. They were covered with a thin layer of white, icy-cold frost.

"I-I d-d-don't think I've ever b-b-been this c-c-cold before in my l-l-life. Do you think we'll f-f-freeze to death?" asked Michael.

"P-please s-say n-no!" said Patrick.

"I f-feel it getting w-warmer," Daisy said.

"I have n-n-never been that s-s-scared before," said Patrick.

Michael hugged himself. "Yeah, m-me either."

Daisy looked at Patrick and saw his glasses start to drip.

"Hey! You're melting, Patrick!"

He looked at his hands. "Oh! Yes! Yes!"

He jumped up and started dancing in place, patting himself all over.

Daisy and Michal joined him, trying to warm up. After a few minutes, the frost had melted and they had stopped shivering. Once they knew they wouldn't freeze to death, they looked around for a way out.

"Well," Michael said, "we're not in the shed anymore, *that's* for sure."

"How could this have happened?" Patrick asked. "Are we actually *inside* that gumball machine?"

Daisy frowned and nodded. "I think we are."

6 The Gumball World

INSIDE THE GUMBALL MACHINE, Daisy, Patrick, and Michael stood next to each other and looked around.

With her hands on her hips, Daisy shook her head. "Wow! It's freaking me out that we're tiny enough to fit into a gumball machine."

"I know," Michael said. "Me too. We look like miniature people. I hope we don't stay like this."

Patrick ran his hands through his hair. "What if we do?" he asked. "Oh, man. My mom will be *so* mad if I have to stay this size. My glasses are even bigger now than they were before."

Daisy's tummy felt funny. She wiped a tear from her eye and looked at her two friends. "How could we be this little?"

Michael shook his head. "It *has* to be magic. It's the *only* explanation. I wonder how we'll get out of here." He rubbed his sore elbow. "What if we're stuck here forever?"

"Forever is a long time," Patrick said.

"Don't say that you guys," Daisy said. "We *have* to get out of here!"

Patrick made a funny, whining noise and walked over to the lid that had slammed shut after they flew through it.

"I know," he said. "We'll just crawl through this opening and slide back down." He grunted as he tried to pull it up. "If we can just—get this—thing to open."

He pulled and grunted and groaned, but it wouldn't budge.

"Come on you guys, help me," he said.

Daisy and Michael joined him, each grabbing a section of the handle, and pulling as hard as they could.

"How could it be so tight? We just came through here," Patrick said.

His great idea was no longer looking that great.

"I don't know," Michael said, "but we *have* to get out of here!" He pounded on the lid.

Patrick stomped on the door and Daisy and Michael joined him. They pulled, pounded, stomped, and kicked the lid, screaming for help, until they were too exhausted to continue and they gave up. Now, instead of shivering, they were sweating and out of breath. The lid was the only way out, and it was *not* opening.

Patrick turned to Daisy and jabbed his finger at her. "This is *your* fault! You just *had* to get that silly red gumball, didn't you? Now, look at us. We're tiny and we're trapped in a gumball machine." His voice got very high. "A *gumball machine* Daisy! No one will *ever* find us in here!"

"Patrick! Get a grip!" Michael shouted. "Freaking out is not going to help us figure out what to do."

Patrick took a couple of deep breaths. "I'm sorry, dude," he said. "You're right. Sorry, Daisy."

"No, *I'm* sorry. *You're* right, Patrick," Daisy said. She felt tears burn her eyes. "This *is* my fault."

As Daisy started to cry, Patrick's lips turned down. He reached a hand up under his glasses and pressed on his eyes.

Michael raised his hands. "Yelling at each other won't get us anywhere. Stop arguing and stop crying. We have to *think*."

He stared at them and waited.

Daisy sniffled. "I'm sorry."

"You're right," Patrick said, nodding.

The three of them started walking, saying nothing for several minutes.

After a while, Patrick stopped and pointed. "Look! I wonder what's over that hill. Maybe there's another way out."

Daisy noticed that the ground looked like dirt, but it wasn't dirt. It was brown and bumpy, with ridges and grooves, which made it easy to climb—but it felt more like rough tree bark—or something.

They reached the hill and Michael was the first to start climbing. Daisy and Patrick followed. Although the hill was a little steep, it wasn't very high. They reached the top in just a few minutes and dropped onto their stomachs to peer over the edge.

"Is this a dream?" asked Patrick.

"I don't know," Michael replied, "but no one will believe this."

"I'm scared," Daisy said.

"Me too," Patrick said. "What in the world is happening to us? I *definitely* want to go home—right now."

They stayed on their stomachs for a long time, watching and trying to understand what they were seeing.

Michael smiled. "Amazing!"

"Yeah," Patrick said. "It looks like a miniature city!"

"This is *so* cool!" Daisy said. "Look at the purple grass and colorful trees. How could this be possible?" she asked.

"I don't get it," Patrick said. "I thought we were inside a gumball machine. Why aren't we surrounded by gumballs?" He pointed. "Are those *buildings* down there?"

"I think so," said Michael. "It looks like a city, or a town or something. But, what are those–things–moving over there?"

In the distance, they saw, what looked like, moving rocks–small and round. Daisy turned and smiled at the boys and then looked back at the weird world.

Michael shrugged his shoulders. "Come on. Let's check it out."

He stood and started walking down the hill.

"Wait! What do you mean–'let's go check it out'? Are you crazy? This could be dangerous," Patrick said.

Michael threw up his hands. "Come on, Patrick. Whatever–or *whoever*–those things are down there, they might be able to help us find our way out. Let's go." Then he laughed. "Besides, how can they hurt us? We're probably ten times bigger than they are."

"Well, we're not as big as we *used* to be," Patrick grumbled. "I'll follow behind you."

Michael slapped Patrick on the back. "Dude–this could be the best adventure ever!"

They walked toward what they thought was some type of city. There were roads that traveled in circles, round houses, and trees with round, colorful gumballs mixed in with the leaves–sort of like flowers. There were many different colors, but almost everything had the same shape–round.

Despite being afraid, the three kids couldn't help but notice what a warm, friendly, and colorful place this was. They still had trouble believing they were *inside* that old gumball machine. They walked up a small hill and stopped to rest.

"Hey," said Daisy. "Look at all those gumballs down there! Let's check it out!"

She started walking down the hill, but Patrick grabbed her arm.

"Maybe we should stay behind this tree–or whatever it is, and check things out for a minute–you know–and see what's out there before *it* sees *us*."

"That's a good idea," Michael whispered.

They hid behind some round bushes, pushing aside leaves and gumballs to get a better look. Daisy looked up and smiled. An orange gumball hung on a leaf just above her and she reached for it. Patrick grabbed her hand.

"Are you *kidding* me, Daisy? Remember the last time you wanted a gumball? Do you really think you should be doing that *again*? We might turn into a gumball and *stay* a gumball forever. So–please–do *not* eat these, okay?"

"Okay, okay. Yes. You're right. Sorry. Excellent thinking," said Daisy, frowning. "Anyway, I still have that red one in my mouth. See?"

She blew a huge bubble and popped it.

Patrick glared at her. "*Seriously?* Are you *still* chewing that? You realize that that's probably why we're here, don't you? Because you ate a one-hundred-year-old gumball!"

"It tastes fine," Daisy said.

Patrick frowned and shook his head.

"Stop arguing!" Michael whispered. "Look! Those gumballs are moving!"

Daisy chewed her gumball loudly, just to irritate Patrick. She nodded and smiled. "So cool, right? It looks like they're talking and laughing!"

"This is a nightmare," said Patrick. "What *are* those things?"

"I think they're like–gumball people–or something," Daisy said. "I'm not really sure."

"That's what it looks like," Michael said. "Look! They have two eyes, a nose, a mouth, two short little arms, and two feet."

Daisy giggled. "Just like us!"

"Well, not *exactly* like us," Patrick said. "I mean, where are their legs? It doesn't look like they have any, which is totally weird."

"Oh, you're right," Daisy said. "*Very* weird."

"Seriously," Patrick said. "Are we dreaming? I mean, this *can't* be real."

"I have no idea," Daisy said. "Let's see." She reached out and pinched his arm.

"Ooh-owie! Hey!"

Patrick gave Daisy a dirty look as he rubbed his arm.

"Nope. We're not dreaming," she said. "This is *real* and we need to figure out what to do. Now quit asking that question."

"Well, you don't have to *yell* at me and pinch me—and—wrinkle my shirt," Patrick said, smoothing his sleeve.

Daisy opened her mouth to yell back at Patrick when Michael interrupted them.

"Stop it you guys! We're in a lot of trouble here and we need to find out how to get home. We can't do that if you two waste time arguing."

Daisy sighed. "You're right. Sorry."

"Okay, okay," Patrick said, rubbing his sore arm.

They turned their attention back to the strange looking gumball creatures.

"I wonder if those gumball people—or whatever they are—talk," Michael said.

Daisy laughed. "Oh right. Talking gumballs. Now I've heard everything."

"Well, look at them," Michael said.

"Yeah, and maybe they eat *people* in their world, just like people in our world eat *gumballs*," Patrick said.

Michael nodded and looked back at the gumball creatures. "Yeah, and maybe they don't even swallow them. Maybe they just chew them up and spit them out, like we do with gumballs," he said.

Daisy frowned. "Either way, it would *not* be good for us, would it?"

Michael and Patrick shook their heads.

They continued watching the gumball people from behind the gumball bushes.

"It's unreal," Daisy said. "Those creatures have *so* many different colors. I've never seen so many."

"My favorite," said Patrick, "are the ones that have a mixture of colors swirled around their bodies."

"I like the turquoise ones," Michael said.

"Yes," Daisy said. "And look—there are maroon ones, hot pink, and even violet colored gumballs."

Violet.

She turned to the boys. "You guys—I almost forgot—today's my birthday! I *really* don't want to spend it trapped inside an old gumball machine. I want to go home. My parents are going to freak out if I'm not there for my party."

Michael looked at her and patted her shoulder. "Come on, Daisy. This might be the best birthday of your life."

Patrick rubbed his hands through his hair. "I'm with Daisy," he said. "The sooner we find our way out of here, the better."

They watched the gumball people for a few more minutes, and then Michael stood up.

"Come on," he said. "Maybe those funny-looking gumball people can help us find our way out of here."

They walked down the hill toward the gumball town. Patrick's foot had fallen asleep, so he shook it and stomped it while Daisy and Michael watched.

"Dude," Michael said, laughing. "You look like Frankenstein."

A tiny giggle slipped from Daisy's mouth, but she quickly covered it with her hand. "Sorry, Patrick."

Patrick grumbled as he hopped and stomped his way down the hill. The bumpy road led them toward the mysterious city, and when they came to a round sign on a pole, they looked up to read it.

"Pink Street," said Patrick.

They looked at each other.

"Interesting," said Michael.

"I think it's cute," said Daisy.

Patrick rolled his eyes. "Oh, brother."

"Yeah, really Daisy. What's with you and pretty colors lately? Are you turning into a *girl* or something?" asked Michael. He gave her a small shove.

Daisy stopped and stomped her foot. "In case you two haven't noticed, I *am* a girl!"

"Shh! Keep your voices down! The gumballs will hear you," whispered Patrick.

Daisy folded her arms and looked Patrick in the eye. "Oh, really? How do you know they can *hear* anything?"

Michael put up his hands. "Just stop it, you two. Keep it down, and keep walking."

The three kids headed down Pink Street. As they walked, they saw gumball houses, trees, parks, dogs, cats, birds, and many gumball people.

"Yep," Patrick said. "They're *definitely* gumball people."

"Yep," Michael said.

"They don't look *too* scary," Daisy said. "Right?"

The boys frowned.

"Hard to tell," Michael said. "We won't know until we get down there."

The houses on Pink Street (and on Blue Street, Red Street, Green Street, and Yellow Street) were round and curvy. Each house had two windows and a door, and each house and door was a different color from the next. The front yards were very colorful, and each had a curvy sidewalk shaped like an "s" leading to the front door. Every yard had cheerful and colorful gumball flowers planted in the purple grass that bordered the walkways and edges of the houses.

The trees appeared to be some kind of fruit tree, but Daisy and the boys weren't sure what kind of fruit tree would have so many different colors of fruit on one tree. When they took a closer look, they noticed that it wasn't fruit. The tree was covered with gumballs—of course. Gumballs were everywhere!

Michael looked up and pointed. "Wow! Check out that sky!"

"Cool! It's pink and purple!" Patrick said.

Daisy smiled. "Pretty."

For the first time since arriving, she felt the butterflies in her tummy disappear.

The boys looked at her and rolled their eyes. They both knew it was pretty, but boys never say stuff like that out loud. That would be very *un*cool.

"And look! A rainbow!" Patrick shouted.

In the sky off to their right, was a huge, bright rainbow. Everything was so colorful and cheerful. Daisy watched Patrick's face change. His eyes were bright and his smile grew. She knew he was finally starting to relax, just as she was.

As they walked closer to the houses, they were able to see what the gumball people really looked like. They were everywhere!

There were mother gumballs holding their baby gumballs, father gumballs playing catch with their gumball children, and there were children gumballs throwing baseballs, and playing football. Some gumballs were even swinging on swing sets.

Even though Daisy, Patrick, and Michael had shrunk in size, the gumballs were quite small in comparison. Most of the gumball people only came up to the children's waists, and they waddled like a duck when they walked. Daisy figured that was because they didn't have legs. They only had feet. It must be hard to walk with no legs, she thought. It didn't seem to matter to them, though. The gumball people seemed happy!

In the distance, the children noticed some smaller gumball people playing catch in a park. They were throwing something that looked like a football or a baseball. However, as the children approached the group, they saw that it wasn't just any kind of ball they were throwing. They were throwing tiny gumball children, who giggled as they were tossed into the air. Sometimes they were caught, and other times they were dropped, but the hard landing didn't seem to bother them. They just rolled back up and giggled some more, as they ran to the back of a long line of gumball children waiting for their turn to be thrown.

"Did you see that?" Patrick asked. "How could they do that to those little gumballs?"

"Yeah," Michael said. "And why aren't they getting hurt when they're dropped?"

"I don't get it," Daisy said, shaking her head.

Off to Daisy's left, she saw two gumballs walking toward them. One gumball was white, and one gumball was black, and they were larger than the other gumball people.

"Uh-oh. You guys," whispered Daisy, as she nudged Michael's arm. "We have company."

7 Gumble and Gumba

THE BOYS LOOKED PAST DAISY and watched the two large gumball people walking toward them.

"You guys," Patrick whispered. "What should we do? They look mad."

"Stay cool," Michael said. "Let's see what they have to say."

The black gumball was the first to approach them. His shell was perfectly round—almost fat. He had big, round, white eyes with pointed white eyebrows. His mouth was white and straight and he had thin, white arms, and large white hands and feet.

"Is he wearing a belt?" Daisy asked.

"I think so," Michael said.

Daisy didn't understand the white belt around his waist, since he wore no pants—or any clothing, for that matter. Maybe his shiny black shell *was* his outfit. She guessed that his shell was made out of delicious sugar.

As he approached, Daisy noticed that the black gumball was just a little bit shorter than they were.

He looked at the kids and said, "Can I help you? Who are you?"

Daisy lifted her hand and gave him a wimpy wave. "Hi. My name is Daisy."

His eyes made her nervous, so she looked at the ground.

Patrick nudged Daisy with his elbow. "Oh, and these are my friends, Patrick and Michael," she said.

The black gumball scrunched his face and wrinkled his nose. "I don't mean to be rude, but 'um—well—what are you doing here? How did you get here?" he asked. "We don't usually have guests—well, actually—you are our *first* guests."

Pointing upward, the black gumball then said, "Oh, wait. Don't tell me. You're from out there."

The children were too afraid to look up. Instead, they nodded.

The white gumball had more of an oval shape. So, because he was longer and thinner, he was much taller than the black gumball. He had round black eyes that pointed upward, near their outside corners, and black eyebrows that were high above his eyes. They made him look happy. His arms, hands, and feet were also black.

He gave the children an angry look and said, "I suppose you think you can come in here and try to chew us up and spit us out like you do with other gumballs. Well, that doesn't work in here," he growled. His voice was lower and scarier than the black gumball's voice.

He raised his fists. "So, if that's your plan, you can bet you'll have a big fight on your hands."

Michael raised his hands. "Oh, no sir! We're not here to do that," he said. "We're here by mistake. We didn't *try* to come in here."

Patrick let out a weak little giggle. "Yes–sir. And, and, and ..."

Daisy shook her head and helped Patrick finish his sentence. "We were afraid that *you* might eat *us*," she said.

Patrick put his hands in his pockets and then pulled them back out. He smiled and kicked some dirt. "That's what I was going to say. Yes."

The black gumball made a noise–like a grunt–and then started to chuckle. He looked over at the white gumball, who joined him.

"Now *that's* funny. You thought *we* would eat *you*? We don't eat humans. That's what you are, right? Humans?"

The children nodded.

The black gumball stopped laughing and said, "You do know we're gumballs, don't you? And you do know that gumballs don't eat humans, right?"

The children nodded. Then Daisy said, "Well–er–yes, sir. We know that. We–ah–you know–we're in your machine–or world or–wherever we are–and we thought that things might be the other way around. I mean, this is our first time actually *inside* a gumball machine, so we're not really sure how things work."

The two gumballs looked at each other and smiled. Patrick let out a loud puff of air, and everyone giggled.

"Well, then," said the smiling, white gumball. "Let's start over." He stuck out his hand. "Hello! My name is Gordy Gumble."

He gave each of the kids a rough handshake.

He turned to the black gumball. "And this is my very good friend, Vinnie Gumba."

"Welcome to the Gumball World!" Vinnie shouted, shaking their hands and smiling.

Gordy laughed. "Like I said, we don't have many visitors, so this is very exciting for us!"

"What do you mean, Gordy? We *never* have visitors!" Vinnie said, laughing. "This is our first time."

"Oh, yes. You're right, Vin," Gordy said.

The laughing slowed and everyone was quiet as the two large gumballs stared at the children. Patrick wrinkled his face and scratched his head as he looked at Daisy and Michael.

"Oh, I'm *so* sorry," said Gordy. "We don't mean to stare. You just look so *strange*."

He turned to Vinnie who nodded. "Yes, it's true. I mean, I've never seen anything like you before."

Vinnie and Gordy stared some more. The children said nothing, but continued to smile and nod while the two talking gumballs looked them over.

Finally, Gordy clapped his hands and smiled. "I'm forgetting my manners. I hope you'll forgive me," he said. "Please—come with us. Meet our families!"

"Yes," Vinnie said, "and perhaps you'd care to join us in a friendly game of football."

Patrick jumped up and down and said, "Sure! That sounds fun!"

Michael smiled and slapped Daisy on the back. "We'd love to, wouldn't we Daisy?"

As soon as Vinnie and Gordy turned their backs, Daisy gave Michael a nasty look as she swung her hand out to hit him. She missed, and Michael laughed.

"Thanks a lot," she whispered.

After that, the kids were quiet as they followed the two gumballs down Pink Street.

Gordy gave the children a tour as they walked along the curving, winding road.

"As you'll see when we get closer to town," he said, "Vinnie and I are a little bigger and much older than most of the other gumballs."

"Yes," Vinnie said. "That's because, in the beginning, black and white gumballs were the only ones in this world."

"It was *pretty* boring, as you can imagine," said Gordy.

"Yep! Pretty boring," said Vinnie.

"Anyway," Gordy continued, "as time passed, we started getting gumballs with other colors. For a long time, it would rain gumballs whenever a human from your world poured a bunch of them into the top of the machine. We made many new and interesting friends, and we were excited to see our world turn from boring old black and white to something so colorful and beautiful! But lately, things have slowed down. We haven't had any new arrivals in quite a while."

"I'll bet it's because the machine is sitting in a dirty old shed. It looks like no one has paid any attention to it in years," Daisy said.

"That must be why you're not getting any new gumballs," said Michael. "I don't think anyone cares about it anymore."

"Hmm. That's very interesting," said Vinnie.

"Well, we won't be losing any of the ones we have now, since no one will be using the machine," said Gordy.

This made Daisy think about the red gumball she was still chewing. *Uh-oh.*

She immediately stopped moving her mouth. She didn't want Gordy or Vinnie to see her chewing one of their friends. She pretended to cough and covered her mouth. As she did this, she spit the piece of gum into her hand and then put it in her pocket. She knew her mom would be upset about her putting sticky, chewed-up gum in her pocket, but she'd worry about that later.

Gordy saw her spit out the gum. He smiled and said, "Don't worry. You're not actually chewing one of us."

Daisy's eyes opened wide as she covered her mouth.

"That's true," Vinnie said. "Most of the gumballs that come in here are plain gumballs. They don't talk or live with us, so that's what we call them. We try to stay in the middle and keep the plain ones up against the walls. We push them to the outside edges of our world, and they're usually the ones that go down when the crank is turned. We call that a shakedown."

"What's a shakedown?" asked Patrick.

"Oh, my," Gordy said. "It's hard to describe, but it's sort of like an earthquake because the whole world starts vibrating and shaking. You'll know it when it happens. You'll *feel* it."

"Do you have a lot of shakedowns?" asked Michael.

"Well, I wouldn't say a *lot* of them," Vinnie said. "It happens when a coin is inserted into the slot. We had four or five shakedowns a little while ago."

"Yes," Gordy said. "That must have been you, inserting your coins. Do you know who owns this machine?"

"Nope," said Michael. "We found it sitting in the shed. I don't think anyone else will be using it for a long time."

Daisy, Patrick, and Michael looked at each other.

"You guys," Daisy said. "No one knows where we are."

"You're right," Patrick said. "Who would think to look for us inside an old gumball machine?"

Michael nodded. "That's the *last* place anyone would ever check."

"Don't worry," Gordy said. "Hopefully, someone will come along and put in a coin."

"Yes," Vinnie said, "and if they don't, we'll figure something out. We won't let you stay stuck up here. Please don't worry. And remember, we *love* getting newcomers."

Gordy giggled. "Of course, our newcomers are usually gumballs, but it's extra nice having you humans here for a visit, too. Life is so much more fun when you can make new friends, isn't it?"

Vinnie smiled and nodded. "So true."

"They're right," Michael said. "Let's go meet some new friends. I don't want to worry about how we'll get home. We'll figure that out later."

"I sure hope you're right," Patrick said. "Daisy has a birthday party in a few hours."

Daisy thought about her party and about Violet. She had a feeling that they'd become good friends. She smiled.

If we ever get out of here, I'll invite her to my party.

"What are you smiling about?" asked Michael.

"Oh, nothing. I'll tell you later," she said. Michael shrugged and turned to Vinnie and Gordy.

Vinnie continued, "I'm sure we'll figure something out, but a shakedown would be the best thing. I'm sure that you humans can't survive on gumballs, so I do hope someone comes upon the gumball machine very soon."

Daisy thought Vinnie didn't sound very hopeful, and after that, everyone was quiet for a moment.

"Hey, I just thought of something," Patrick interrupted. "Our bikes! They're sitting right there in the alley. Maybe someone will see them and look for us."

Through his glasses, Daisy thought she saw Patrick's eyes twinkle.

"Yes," she said, "but even if they found our bikes, that doesn't mean they'll go into the shed, get an urge for a dirty old gumball, and then actually decide to insert a nickel."

"Why not? You did," said Patrick.

She nodded. "That's true."

Michael shook his head. "No. This is *not* good. You guys, we could be stuck here forever."

"Come on," Patrick said. "We have to think. Daisy, it's your birthday today. It won't be long before your parents start to wonder where you are. They'll *have* to start looking for us. Maybe one of your brothers—Joe—or even little Sammie—will find our bikes. And you never know—they might want an old gumball. If they do, I sure hope they'll have a nickel in their pocket."

"Yeah, that could happen, I suppose," Michael said. "But, it's a stretch."

Daisy quietly prayed for one of her brothers to come through for them, but she did worry that the same thing might happen to Joe or Sammie if they put a nickel into that gumball machine. Maybe, they too would get sucked in. If that happened, they'd be doomed for sure.

Vinnie took Daisy's hand and looked at her and the boys. "Today, it was your arrival that shook our world," he said. "We often wonder what it would be like out in your world, but we don't want to be chewed up and spit out, so we stay here. It's a nice place. You'll see."

"Yes," said Gordy. "We don't know how you'll get out, but I'm confident you will. Don't worry about it right now. We have a lot of fun here. Come on. See for yourselves!"

8 The Gumball Party

AS THE GROUP TURNED ONTO YELLOW STREET, they heard a thumping sound in the distance. The children looked at each other but didn't speak. There were trees on either side of the street and they couldn't see past them. As they walked, the sound became louder.

"Is that music I'm hearing?" Daisy asked.

Gordy smiled and nodded. "It is!"

They passed the trees, and an open area of green and purple grass and wild gumball flowers came into view. In the grass, Daisy saw, at least, fifty colorful gumball people, small and large, all dancing together, and laughing and singing.

Daisy giggled. "It's a party!"

The children followed Vinnie and Gordy as they walked up to the group. The music stopped and the gumballs turned and stared at their new visitors. The silence echoed over the hills. Never before had Daisy felt so uncomfortable.

Why are they staring at us?

She realized the gumballs must think she, Patrick, and Michael looked strange.

"Boy, are we out of place here," said Patrick.

"Yeah, this is weird," Michael said.

Gordy waved his hands up and down. "It's alright everyone. Meet our new *human* friends. Don't worry. Continue with your party!"

Daisy thought Gordy must be the leader because the gumball people seemed to trust him. They listened to him and went back to their party.

It didn't take long for Daisy and the boys to relax and enjoy themselves, too. They watched and tapped their feet. This was a new kind of dancing they'd never seen.

"These gumballs really know how to shake and boogie, don't they?" Patrick shouted over the loud music. Daisy and Michael nodded.

Michael laughed. "They look really funny dancing without legs."

"Yeah, and we'd break a leg doing some of the stuff they're doing," Patrick said.

Some of the gumballs bounced off the walls to the beat of the music. Others bounced off each other. There was one pink gumball that always had one eye closed as if she was winking. Daisy made up a name for her–Pinkie Winkie.

Pinkie Winkie rolled around like a ball, laughing and giggling. Daisy, Michael, and Patrick cheered her and the others on as everyone moved and swayed, and clapped their hands to the beat.

"I really want to get out there," said Patrick.

Daisy was about to tell him not to, but it was too late.

"Watch this," he said.

He walked out into the middle of the group, and soon, a bunch of little gumballs surrounded him, their heads only as high as his waist.

Daisy looked at Michael with a frown. "Oh, boy–he's not going to do the robot again, is he?"

Before Michael could respond, Patrick did just that. He started with the robot and then added a little break-dancing. He saved the best for last–a little hip-hop and then–the big finisher–the worm!

Daisy had to admit he was a very good dancer. The little gumballs seemed to enjoy his moves and even started to mimic some of them. Daisy thought they looked so cute–and funny–trying to do those moves with their little round bodies.

As they watched Patrick's show, Michael suddenly found himself buckled at the knees, falling into the dancing crowd. A blue gumball had rolled up behind him and rammed him-hard.

"Come on. Show us what you've got," said the blue gumball.

"No, no. I can't dance," Michael replied as he staggered to his feet.

Daisy laughed and gave him a little push. "Go on, Michael. Show them how it's done. Break it down."

Wiping his hands on his pants, Michael said, "Okay. *You* asked for it."

He walked onto the dance floor and did some of the worst dancing Daisy had ever seen. He jerked and slid his feet, and rolled his body forward and then backward.

She shook her head and laughed. "What are you doing?"

Michael smiled and kept dancing.

Daisy giggled and ran out to join them. She held the hands of two little gumballs and, as they rolled, she jumped over them. The gumballs laughed and jumped and moved closer to Michael, Patrick, and Daisy so they could get a better look at their hilarious human dance moves.

"Look, they're laughing at *us*! Can you believe that? *We're* the only ones doing it right," Patrick shouted to Daisy and Michael over the loud music.

Daisy laughed. "Well, maybe they think *they're* doing it right."

The dancing and partying lasted for an hour until everyone got tired.

Gordy put his arms around Daisy and Patrick while Michael put his hands on his knees and tried to catch his breath.

"It looks like you kids have had enough dancing for a while," Gordy said. "Why don't we head over to my house so you can relax and unwind?"

The kids nodded. "Sure," Daisy said. "That sounds nice."

"Great," he said. "I'd like you to meet my family. We'll have something to eat, and then maybe, after a while, we could play a friendly game of football."

Daisy gave him her best fake smile and a thumbs-up. Michael had to cover his mouth to keep from laughing.

"Football sounds fun, doesn't it Dais'?"

She gave Michael a small shove, and he laughed.

Daisy, Patrick, and Michael said goodbye to their new gumball friends, high-fiving them as they left. They started on their way to Gordy's house. Vinnie came with because he wanted to introduce the children to his family, too.

Gordy waved them along. "Vinnie's house won't be out of our way," he said, "because the Gumbas live right next door to the Gumbles."

9 Pudding Hill

THE KIDS FOLLOWED VINNIE AND GORDY to Yellow Street and walked a very long time before seeing much of anything. There were no trees, houses, or gumball people. The grass was sort of brown and ugly, and there were just a few plain gumballs scattered about.

After a while, Daisy noticed that Gordy and Vinnie had started walking faster. She struggled to keep up with them, and then, she saw them start to roll—like balls. Soon, they were rolling super-fast!

Running was more difficult for the children than it normally was because their legs were so tired from their shrinking-freezing-getting-sucked-up-the-tunnel journey that brought them up and into the gumball machine.

Daisy did a slow jog next to Michael and Patrick. "What are they doing?" she asked. "Why are they rolling so fast?"

"I don't know," said Patrick. "That must be their way of running or something. Remember, they don't have any legs."

"Oh, right. That makes sense," she said. "But what's the big hurry? Why are they running—I mean—rolling? Is something chasing them? We don't even know if we should be afraid. Do you think we should be afraid?"

"I have no idea," Michael said. "But I sure wish they'd slow down. I can't keep up. My legs feel like cement."

Daisy turned to look back in case something might be chasing Vinnie and Gordy.

"There's nothing coming," she said. "This is weird. I mean, look at them go!"

The children watched Gordy and Vinnie up ahead of them, as they rolled at lightening-speed.

Daisy called out to them. "You guys! Wait! Why are you rolling so fast? Gordy! Vinnie! Wait for us!"

She and the boys started running faster. Her legs felt heavy, but she didn't want to lose sight of them.

Gordy turned back to look at the children. "Come on! It's Pudding Hill! You'll love it!"

Daisy was out of breath as she shouted to him. "I can't hear you! *Near the hill*? Did you say '*near the hill*,' Gordy?"

She turned to the boys jogging next to her. "It sounded like he said '*near the hill*.' What does that mean?"

"I have no clue," Patrick said, panting.

Vinnie and Gordy rolled around and around—with their heads up, and then their feet up—then back down—up—and then back down.

Vinnie shouted back, "You'll see!"

But his voice trailed off each time his face rolled toward the ground.

Turning to the others, Patrick said, "Did he say, 'you bee'? 'Your knee'? I can't understand him! What the heck is he saying to us?"

Michael and Daisy shook their heads and kept jogging.

The three kids tried hard to keep up, but the two gumballs kept rolling at top speeds. As they rounded a curve, Daisy and the boys saw Gordy drop down and disappear. Then, Vinnie dropped and disappeared, too.

The kids stopped and looked at each other.

"Whoa!" said Daisy.

"Where did they go?" asked Michael.

"They just—disappeared," said Patrick.

"Wait … listen," whispered Daisy. "I hear something."

They stood quietly—listening.

"I don't hear anything," said Michael. "What are we listening for?"

"Shh! There it is again," Daisy said. "Did you hear it?"

Patrick grabbed Daisy's arm. "Yes! I hear it!"

They started walking toward it. After a short distance, they noticed the road came to an abrupt end. It dropped off—like a cliff. Slowly, they inched their way to the edge.

"Do you think they fell all the way down and hurt themselves?" asked Michael.

"I don't know," said Patrick. "I sure hope not."

"D-a-i-s-y! M-i-c-h-a-e-l! P-a-t-r-i-c-k! We're down here!"

The voice came from far below, but they couldn't see anyone. The bottom was so far down it made the children dizzy. They stepped back a few feet so they were safely away from the edge.

"They *did* fall. They need us to help them!" cried Patrick. "I hope they're not hurt. What should we do?"

Daisy turned to the boys. "One of you should crawl to the edge and look down there—but be careful."

"*I'm* not going to the edge. *You* go to the edge," Patrick said.

Daisy folded her arms. "*I'm* not going to the edge."

Michael put his hands on his hips. "Fine," he said. "*I'll* go." He stomped his feet as he walked toward the edge. "What a bunch of chickens."

As Michael started walking, the edge of the cliff came up sooner than he'd expected, and he slipped. He felt himself fall and screamed as he tried to grab something to catch himself, but it was too late.

"Oh my gosh, Patrick—he fell! Come on!"

Michael managed to grab a branch and he hung on tight. His feet dangled beneath him as he reached for a rock on top of the cliff.

"Help! You guys, I'm falling! Help!" He didn't want to look down, but he couldn't help it.

"We're coming, Michael! Hang on!" Daisy shouted.

"Be careful!" Michael yelled from below the cliff. "The edge comes up fast!"

His hand slipped from the rock and branch. He moaned as he struggled to hang on.

Daisy and Patrick knelt down and grabbed his arms. Michael grunted, panted, and kicked, as he tried to find something to brace his feet. His kicking caused rocks and gravel to come loose and fall far below. He slipped and dropped a little, and the three of them screamed. Daisy and Patrick saw the fear in Michael's eyes as they fought to pull him up.

"Don't drop me you guys! Please!"

"Hang on Michael!" Patrick yelled.

They pulled and pulled until he was finally over the edge and safe. After a minute of heavy breathing, the three kids heard a distant voice calling from below.

"What are you guys *doing* up there? Come on down! Don't do it the way Michael just did or you'll never get down here! You have to *run*!"

Too afraid to walk to the edge, the kids turned onto their stomachs and crawled to see who was shouting at them. Whoever it was, he sure must have been a long way down, because they could barely hear him.

As they reached the edge, they looked down. Far below, they saw Gordy and Vinnie looking up and waving at them. They were so far down, that they looked like tiny grains of salt. Patrick noticed something off to their right.

He pointed. "Hey! What's that? It looks like a slide."

It was coated with something shiny and pink, and it started just below where Michael had fallen.

"Wow! Where'd *that* come from?" asked Michael.

They hadn't seen it before because of some tree branches in the way. The slick, pink slide traveled around and around, down to the bottom, where there was a pond filled with what looked like pink goo. They pulled themselves off their stomachs and sat up.

Daisy smiled. "That must be the pudding! Oh, *now* I get it. Gordy didn't say *'near the hill."* He said *Pudding Hill.* This is Pudding Hill!" she said.

"Are we supposed to go down that slide?" Patrick asked, wringing his hands.

"I think so," said Daisy.

Patrick shook his head and whined. "I can't take much more of this. I've been more afraid this morning than I've been in my whole life!"

Michael turned to the other two and said, "Do you mean to tell me I thought I almost killed myself going over that edge when those two *goofballs* down there could have just told us about the slide? I'm going to …"

"Shh! Someone's coming!" Daisy whispered.

They turned and saw some smaller gumball people–two purple ones, an orange one, and a turquoise one–laughing and rolling toward them.

"Hi!" said the turquoise gumball. "Come on down Pudding Hill. It's a blast–and it's bubblegum flavored. Try it!"

"Yes, try it," added one of the purple gumballs.

They didn't stop to see if the children were coming. Instead, they rolled up to the edge and jumped. They screamed and laughed as they rolled like bowling balls down the slide.

The orange one, who was the last one to jump, said, "Don't forget to take a good running start before you go, or else you won't make it all the way down. You'll just stop right in the middle of the slide."

Then, he too, was gone, disappearing over the edge.

"Wait a minute, wait a minute," said Patrick to Michael and Daisy. "It's bad enough that we have to go down this *gigantic* slide, but I am *not* making a running start for it, too. I mean, it's like jumping to my death. I just *cannot* do it. It's too scary!"

Michael put his hand on Patrick's shoulder. "Dude. You heard that orange gumball. You *have* to run or you'll stop halfway down. Do you *want* to be stuck halfway down?"

"No, but—my glasses. I'll lose my glasses. I'll be in big trouble if I lose them."

"Now you're just making excuses, Patrick," Daisy said. "We're *already* in big trouble just by *being* in this gumball machine. This is no time to worry about your glasses."

Michael nodded. "I don't think we have a choice. I don't want to be stuck up here when everyone else is down there. Who wants to go first?"

No one said anything. They just looked at each other.

Michael threw up his arms. "Are you *kidding* me?"

He huffed and stomped his feet and kicked some dirt. "Fine. Fine! I guess I'll go first, even though I just fell over this cliff five seconds ago. I have to do everything!"

He took a deep breath and ran his fingers through his hair.

Daisy smiled. She knew they had nothing to worry about. They would be *just* fine. The gumballs would never let them get hurt.

To tease Michael, she giggled and said, "Make sure you get that good running start."

He frowned. "You're hilarious, Daisy."

He peered over and looked at the slide. "I just wish that slide was a little bit wider."

He turned and walked past Daisy and Patrick, going far enough to give himself a good running start.

"I think it was made for people without legs," Patrick added.

"Yes, so land in a sitting position, and keep your feet together and your arms at your sides," Daisy said.

Michael nodded. "Right. Okay. Here—I—g-o-o-o!"

He ran past Daisy and Patrick and leaped into the air, disappearing over the cliff as quickly as Vinnie, Gordy, and the others had. Patrick and Daisy looked at each other and smiled.

"Wow," said Daisy. "I can't believe he actually did it."

Patrick's smile fell. "Yeah, me either."

Daisy put her hands on her hips and looked around. I guess one of us has to go next."

They looked at each other and nodded as they slowly walked to the edge and looked down. They could see and hear Michael going down the slide but they couldn't tell if they were hearing screams of laughter or screams of fear.

"I'm glad he landed on the slide in one piece. That's a relief," said Daisy.

"Yep," said Patrick. "That's good."

They stared down at the hill but neither of them was ready to make the jump.

* * * *

MICHAEL LANDED HARD ONTO THE SLIDE, relieved he didn't fall off. He reminded himself to keep his feet and hands inside.

Racing down at lightning speed, he felt the wind whipping his face. He screamed in a high voice, like a little girl in kindergarten.

"Ahh!"

He looked down below his feet and saw a giant dip in the slide.

Uh-oh!

He felt himself dip—up—and then back down. After that, he was going straight down. His arms flew above his head and his stomach seemed to jump into his throat.

"Ahh!"

Michael was moving so fast, he had trouble staying on the slide. It felt like he was riding just above it. He bounced and landed hard, over and over, all the way down.

As the slide began twisting and turning, Michael found himself enjoying the ride. His screams of fear changed to screams of laughter.

"Whoo-h-o-o!"

This isn't so bad, he thought, as he screamed and laughed. He swirled around another bend and saw the end of the slide quickly approaching. He braced himself for the sudden drop-off. He could see the bright pink pond of bubblegum pudding and Vinnie and Gordy smiling and clapping. He hoped the pudding pond wasn't too shallow.

"Here—I—go-o-o!"

He flew up and then felt himself drop. Landing feet first, his body bent forward, slapping the top, and he plunged deep into the pool of pudding. When he came up for air, Vinnie and Gordy were standing waist-deep in the pond waiting for him. They laughed as they gave him high-fives and patted him on the back.

"Congratulations," said Gordy. "You did it!"

Michael coughed and choked as he smiled and wiped his face. "Thanks! It was super-fun!"

He looked down at himself and saw that he was covered with thick and gooey pink pudding. He felt it drip down his head and slide into his eyes and mouth. His clothes were heavy and felt warm from the sticky pink slime. He smelled the strong scent of bubblegum as he wiped the pudding away from his eyes.

"Whoo-hoo!" he laughed. "That was one *awesome* ride!"

The gumballs who went down the slide before Michael joined in the celebration. Everyone cheered and congratulated him for braving the ride. He was so happy and proud of himself that he swiped a big glob of bubblegum flavored pudding off his forehead and put it into his mouth. He chewed it up and blew out a *huge* bubble. The place grew quiet as Vinnie, Gordy, and the other gumballs stood and stared at him with their mouths hanging open.

Without thinking, Michael popped his large bubble and felt it smear all over his mouth.

Wiping it off with his hand, he looked around and saw everyone staring at him. "Oops," he said. "Did I just eat one of your friends or something?"

The gumballs continued to stare, and then one of the littler gumballs covered his mouth to hide his giggles.

Vinnie let out a big laugh and smacked Michael on the back. "Nah," he said. "Just messing with you. You didn't eat one of our children if that's what you were thinking."

Michael gave them a nervous smile as he looked around at everyone.

"Don't worry," Gordy said. "This is Grandma Gumble's famous bubblegum pudding recipe. She'll be thrilled that you like it!" He let out a big howling laugh.

"Ha, ha. Very funny," Michael said.

The gumballs kept laughing as they jumped and splashed around in the pudding.

Over their laughter, they heard screaming coming from above and turned to look up at the slide. Daisy was racing down, heading straight for them. Her hair flew wildly around her face, so Michael couldn't tell if she was laughing or crying. He stopped celebrating to make sure she was enjoying the ride. He caught only brief glimpses of her as she came around the curves, but when he did see her, he saw that she was indeed smiling.

Michael laughed and shouted, "Daisy's coming down. Get ready!"

Everyone backed away in time for her to fly off the slide and drop into the pudding pool, landing with a big splash. Her screams were muffled as she plunged deep into the pile of pink goo.

She came up gasping and smiling and dripping with sticky pudding. Coughing and laughing at the same time, she said, "Oh boy! That was amazing!"

The celebration continued for a while until Michael realized that Patrick was still nowhere in sight. Daisy saw Michael looking up and knew something was wrong.

"No sign of Patrick," she said. "He was really afraid to jump, but I thought he was right behind me."

****

AT THE TOP OF THE HILL, seated near the edge of the cliff, Patrick looked down the slide. Even the butterflies in his stomach seemed nervous. He wished he'd have gone down before Daisy because then he'd be down there with Michael right now.

Instead, he was sitting all alone on top of the world—a crazy gumball world—with no one to talk him into going down. Everyone was already down there. He started to cry a little, but was startled by a small gumball child who approached him from behind.

"What's wrong?" she asked.

Patrick turned around to see the small, pink gumball girl, who Daisy had named Pinkie Winkie from the party, standing right behind him.

"I'm really afraid to go down that slide," he said.

"Oh, I know what you mean," said Pinkie Winkie. "I was really scared to go down my first time, too."

Patrick felt himself relax. "You were?"

She nodded. "But my dad told me that being afraid would keep me from trying new and exciting things. He promised me he'd never let me do anything he knew was dangerous. I believed him. And, you know what?"

"What?" asked Patrick.

"He was right. The slide is fun. You won't get hurt. I promise. Go ahead. You'll see. I'll be right behind you."

At that moment, Patrick heard Michael and Daisy's faint voices calling up to him from far below.

He smiled and nodded. "Okay," he said to Pinkie Winkie. "I'll do it!"

"Good. Don't forget to get a good running start," she said.

"How could I forget?" he asked. "I think I've heard that a million times just this morning." He sighed. "Okay. Let's get this over with."

Patrick walked back to where Michael and Daisy had started and took a deep breath.

"See you down there," squeaked Pinkie Winkie.

"Yeah, see you down there."

Patrick paused for a moment to gather his courage, took a deep breath, and started to run. He picked up speed until he was running fast, but when he reached the edge, he abruptly stopped.

"Oh! What's the matter?" asked Pinkie Winkie. "Why did you stop?"

Patrick was out of breath. "I chickened out. I can't do it."

"You *can* do it," she said. "Come on, try it again."

"You're right. I *can do* it."

Patrick took another deep breath and walked back to his starting point, but this time, as he picked up speed and reached the edge, he never stopped. He lifted his legs and jumped. With nothing but air underneath him, he screamed.

"Ahh!"

When he thought he'd never land on solid ground, his body banged onto the slide.

"Ooh-owie! Oh boy, oh boy, oh boy. Here I g-o-o-o!"

At the bottom of the hill, Daisy and Michael heard Patrick's shrieks, but they couldn't see him.

"Well," said Daisy, "now we know he made the jump!"

"Yep!" said Michael.

They watched and waited.

"Ooh! There he is!" shouted Vinnie. "Whoo-hoo! He's coming down the dip! Do you see him?"

Daisy and Michael couldn't see him, but they could hear him.

"Ahh!"

Up on the slide, Patrick's blond hair flew straight above his head. He felt the cool wind slap his cheeks as he flew around the curves, his body swinging up to the right and then up to the left.

Finally, Daisy and Michael could see Patrick, and Patrick could see them. By the time he felt his body launch off the edge, he was smiling. In the air, he kicked and screamed and then belly-flopped into the pink pond of pudding.

When he came up for air, dripping in pink goo, he was greeted by a huge crowd of cheering gumballs and, of course, Michael and Daisy. Like everyone else, Patrick was covered with the sticky stuff, including his glasses. Everyone patted him on the back and congratulated him for facing his fear and doing something new and exciting. Patrick felt wonderful and proud.

After wiping the goo off his glasses so he could see, he looked down at his clothes and frowned.

"Uh-oh. My new shirt! It's ruined," he said, trying to brush away the sticky pudding.

Just then, Pinkie Winkie flew off the slide with a squeaky scream, and landed right on top of Patrick, sending him back down into the pudding.

"So much for trying to clean his shirt," Michael said, laughing.

As Patrick and Pinkie Winkie came up for air, Pinkie Winkie shouted to him. "I told you it was fun!" She jumped up and down, giggling as the gumballs yelled and cheered. They lifted Patrick into the air and bounced him around.

Soon, all three children were tossed in the air and then dropped back into the pudding. During all of the commotion, the gumballs throwing Patrick got a little too close to shore and he landed on the hard ground instead of the pool of pudding.

He sat up and rubbed his back. "Ooh-owie. Not cool, you guys. *Not* cool."

Covering his mouth with his hands, Gordy said, "Oh no! I'm sorry, Patrick!" He ran to help him up. "We're not used to lifting people as big as you are. I guess we were trying too hard."

"This sure has been a rough morning," Patrick said. "You guys are pretty strong for gumballs."

When the celebration was over, the three kids ran under a nearby waterfall to rinse off the sticky pink pudding.

"I sure hope this comes off," Patrick said to Daisy.

Daisy smiled. "I don't think your shirt will ever be the same."

"I don't think *I'll* ever be the same," Patrick said. He couldn't help but smile—just a little.

10 The Game

AFTER THEIR WATERFALL SHOWER, the children had a chance to dry off as they walked to an open field where it looked like a game of football was in progress. Michael and Patrick hoped they could join in and asked Gordy and Vinnie if it was alright.

"Of course," Vinnie said. "Daisy? Would you like to join us"?

"Daisy hates football," Michael said. "She doesn't like to be tackled."

Daisy gave Michael her meanest glare.

"From the looks of that big gumball out there, I'm not so sure I want to play your version of football either," Patrick said.

"Oh, that's just Jawbreaker," Vinnie said. "He's not as rough as he looks."

"Jawbreaker? That's his name?" Michael asked. He frowned as he gave Patrick and Daisy a side-glance.

Jawbreaker was the biggest gumball the children had seen since they arrived inside the gumball machine. He had many swirling colors—yellow, green, red, and blue. His eyebrows were very close together making him look angry all the time.

"Sure, his name is Jawbreaker. Why?" asked Vinnie.

He saw the look of fear on the kids' faces. "Oh, don't worry," he laughed. "He probably won't break your jaws. You're a little too tall for him."

Gordy clapped his hands. "Come on everybody. Let's join the game!"

Vinnie and Gordy rolled ahead, calling out to Jawbreaker.

Daisy folded her arms. "I am *not* playing with that brute," she said.

"Oh, come on, Dais'. We can *take* these guys," Michael said. "I *know* we can. They're smaller than us—and they're *round*! Let's show them how it's done!"

Patrick nodded. "They're just *gumballs*. They don't know how to play football! This'll be fun." He tucked in his damp, sticky shirt and adjusted his glasses. "Let's do this," he said.

As they approached the two teams, Jawbreaker looked up at the children.

He pointed and shouted to Daisy. "You! Come here! You're on my team!"

Daisy felt her legs start to shake and wobble. She looked at the boys hoping they'd rescue her, but they were useless because now they looked afraid, too. She had no choice. She slowly walked over to Jawbreaker's team.

There were six other gumballs standing around Jawbreaker, and they all stared at Daisy as she approached them. She lowered her eyes to the ground, fearful that they would start shouting at her at any moment. Suddenly, a very large green gumball rolled over to Jawbreaker.

"Come on, Jawbreaker. I don't want that *freak* on our team," he said.

Daisy stopped walking and stared at him. She felt as if she'd been kicked in the stomach.

Was he talking about me?

"Oh keep your yap shut, Steeler," Jawbreaker said.

Steeler? Did he just call him Steeler?

Oh, this is great, thought Daisy. I'm playing football—which I hate—with two gigantic gumballs named Jawbreaker and Steeler. And—Steeler thinks I'm a freak. She rubbed her hands together to stop them from shaking.

This should be fun.

"Well, come on, man," Steeler said, "look at her."

Some of the others from the gumball team nodded and stared at her.

"Yeah, we don't want her on our team," said one of them.

Steeler continued. "First of all, she's a *girl*."

A girl? What's wrong with being a girl?

"Second of all," Steeler said, "she has all kinds of strange things going on with her."

Daisy felt the heat rise in her cheeks.

Why won't he stop talking?

"Her coloring is all off," he said. "I mean, what color is she, anyway? It's like—*no* color."

Daisy shook her head and pressed her hands into her stomach.

Now I have no color? What is he talking about?

"Yeah, and look at that stuff coming out of the top of her," said a blue gumball.

"It's called *hair*," Daisy snapped.

"Well, whatever you call it, it's weird," Steeler said. "And, look at her arms. Plus, she can't roll because she's not round. She's so—bumpy. What good is she going to do us?"

Daisy had never been treated so mean. She felt awful standing there listening to them.

She walked closer to Steeler and shook her finger at him as she hooked her lip. "You sure are *mean*. No one has *ever* said such terrible things about me before. Why do you care what I look like? You don't even *know* me. Looks don't matter. I'm a nice person!"

Daisy had no idea where this courage was coming from, but it felt good. She thought about Violet, back home.

Why did she keep thinking about her?

Daisy continued to scold Steeler. She was shouting, but she didn't care. "You must be made of stone, not sweet candy, like most of the *good* gumballs I've met here."

"*Oh*! Steeler! She put you in your place," laughed the blue gumball. "Come with me, young lady. Anyone who stands up to Steeler is a friend of mine."

The blue gumball put his arm around her waist and walked her toward the rest of the team.

"That's enough, Steeler. Now just back off," said Jawbreaker.

"Fine. I still don't like her and I don't want her on my team, but if she has to play with us, I guess there's nothing I can do about it."

Steeler gave Daisy one last dirty look and turned and rolled to the middle of the field.

Jawbreaker rolled up to Daisy. "Don't worry about him. It's too bad some of us up here in the gumball world can't be nice to our visitors."

"It makes me feel bad to have someone treat me like that," Daisy said. "I am a nice person. I don't know why he doesn't like me. I didn't do anything to him. I actually thought everyone liked me. I guess that's not very smart, huh?"

"Well, I don't know how things are where you come from, but up here in the gumball world, there will always be a gumball who doesn't like another gumball just because of the color of his shell," said Jawbreaker. "Some may think their color is prettier, or shinier than another's. It seems silly to me, because, on the inside, all of us gumballs are made out of the same thing—sugar. So, don't let what Steeler said bother you. Just let it roll off your—these things—whatever they are."

Daisy giggled. "They're called *shoulders*."

"Yes, *shoulders*. Just let it roll off your *shoulders*."

"Thanks," she said. "I'll try to remember that."

Wow. For a big, mean looking brute of a gumball, he sure was turning out to be pretty nice. I was wrong to think he'd be mean to me just because he *looked* mean. Daisy felt a little better, but she was still nervous about playing football.

The rest of the team invited her into their huddle. She hadn't been in a huddle since she was seven years old. Somehow, that seemed like a hundred years ago. They whispered their play and gave Daisy her instructions. She prayed she wouldn't get tackled and prayed she wouldn't let her new teammates down—especially, Steeler.

Because Michael and Patrick were not invited onto Jawbreaker's team, they walked over to the other team. The team seemed like a nice bunch of gumballs—until the huddle. Michael and Patrick had never heard such rough-sounding plays! They were worried about Daisy—and themselves. After all, if *these* guys played rough, they could only imagine how rough *Jawbreaker*'s team played.

The two teams lined up for the first play.

"Hut one … hut two."

Daisy and her teammates ran down the field. Jawbreaker had the ball and was looking for someone who was open.

Patrick and Michael started blocking the players on Daisy's team. This wasn't as easy as they'd thought. Her team came at them with full force—like cannonballs!

The gumballs rolled up and grabbed Patrick and Michael by their knees and tackled them. They were down before they knew what hit them. In the meantime, Daisy was doing just what Jawbreaker told her to do—run. When she turned around to see what was happening, she saw the football coming right at her.

"Uh-oh."

She raised her arms and felt the ball ease into her hands.

Wow! I actually caught a football!

A big smile crossed her face as she laughed out loud and turned toward the goal. She picked up speed and zig-zagged around the gumballs rolling toward her. She knew if they grabbed her by the ankles, she'd go down just like Patrick and Michael.

"Please don't let them tackle me! Please don't let them tackle me!"

Behind her, Daisy heard the thunder of little gumballs catching up to her. They sounded like a bunch of bowling balls rolling down the bowling lane all at once.

How could such little guys make so much noise?

She turned her head and saw a couple of bigger gumballs rolling straight for her. She was almost to the end-zone when she heard a crash. She turned to see Jawbreaker knock the last gumball out of her way, and she ran in for a touchdown.

As she crossed the goal line, she jumped up and down. "I did it! I did it!"

Jawbreaker rolled up and high-fived her, as did the rest of her teammates (except for Steeler—he just grumbled and rolled in the other direction).

She ran to Michael and Patrick. "You guys! I did it! I made a touchdown!"

"Good job, Daisy!" Patrick said. "That's awesome!"

Michael smiled and said, "Yeah, Daisy! That was pretty cool! I never knew you could handle a football like that. Maybe you could join us next time we have a game at home."

Daisy nodded and giggled. "Maybe. I might give it a try!"

They played football for another hour, and even though Daisy was tackled a couple of times, she still had fun. Thanks to her new friend, Jawbreaker, Daisy's team won the game.

Afterward, Michael looked at Daisy and smiled. "I still can't believe you *actually* played football, and you *actually* allowed yourself to get tackled."

"Yeah," Patrick said. "And you *actually* got a touchdown. It's a miracle."

"Oh, it's no miracle, you guys," Daisy said. "Now that I know I rock at playing football, you two had better watch out!"

She laughed so hard the two boys couldn't help but laugh, too. They skipped and jumped their way off the field.

After saying goodbye to their new football friends, they left with Vinnie and Gordy to get some lunch at Gordy's house.

11 Meeting The Gumbles

AS THEY WALKED THROUGH THE FRONT DOOR of Gordy's house, Daisy noticed that all of the furniture was round. Across the room, she saw an older-looking gumball woman sitting on a round couch. Daisy thought she looked older because her shell was a little cracked and it looked faded and gray. But the thing Daisy noticed the most about her, was her shape. It was sort of soft-looking, not perfectly round, like the others. The old gumball lady slowly rolled off the couch and headed toward them. As she got closer, she gave Daisy and the boys a hard look and rubbed her hands together.

"Ma," said Gordy, "I'd like you to meet Daisy, Michael, and Patrick. They're the ones from the outside world. Remember? You saw them earlier at the party?"

Gordy's mother gave them a small smile and reached out her hand to welcome them.

"It's a pleasure to meet you," she said, as she looked up at Daisy. "I want to call you children, but you are so *big*. Are you children—or adults—or—giants maybe?" She let out a quiet giggle.

"They're *children*, Mrs. Gumble," said Vinnie.

Some other gumballs came into the living room. Daisy noticed right away that, even though she thought all the gumballs in the gumball world looked alike, these gumballs *really* looked just like Gordy.

"Daisy, Michael, Patrick, I'd like you to meet my wife, Glenda Gumble and our children, Gertrude, Gordy, Jr., and Gilbert Gumble. We are the Gumble family."

"Hi," said Gilbert. He was the smallest of the Gumble children.

Daisy smiled and gave them a small wave. "Hi. It's nice to meet all of you."

After the children were introduced to the Gumble family, everyone sat down for lunch. Daisy and Patrick sat next to each other, and Grandma Gumble asked Michael to sit next to her. Michael gave Patrick and Daisy a nervous look as he walked over and sat in the chair next to her. Patrick and Daisy giggled quietly and then Patrick whispered to Daisy. "Poor Michael. Looks like somebody else thinks he's cute, just like at school!"

Daisy had to cover her mouth to keep the laugh from slipping out.

"You are *so* darling," Grandma Gumble said, "but, if you don't mind my asking, what are these?" She reached over to Michael's thigh and squeezed it hard. Michael held in a groan, as Daisy and Patrick continued to giggle.

"Those are *legs*," answered Michael, rubbing his sore thigh. "We use them to walk and to run."

"Can I try them?" she asked, again reaching for Michael's leg. "No, you can't try them because they don't come off," Michael said.

He looked across the table at Daisy and Patrick and mouthed the word *help*.

"Oh, I see. Sorry."

"That's okay."

"I suppose this doesn't come off either," she said, as she reached over to pinch the skin on Michael's arm.

"Ouch! No. That doesn't come off either—not without a lot of pain," he said, rubbing his arm.

He glanced across the table and saw Daisy and Patrick giggling. "Real funny you guys. Ha ha."

"Oh, I'm so sorry," Grandma Gumble said. "It feels and looks so different. I just wondered what it would look like on me. I thought we could trade."

"Ma, you can't trade his skin for your candy coating. It just doesn't work that way. Now, keep your hands off of him," said Gordy.

Gordy's wife, Glenda, brought a tray of food to the table. On it were gumball sandwiches and gumball chips. For dessert—more pink bubblegum pudding! Everything looked different, but to the three children, it all tasted the same—like gumballs.

12 Sammie

DAISY'S YOUNGER BROTHER, SAMMIE, checked himself out in his bedroom mirror. He had just thrown on a pair of basketball shorts and a T-shirt and was combing his hair. He was glad his blond curls had recently been cut off. He hated those curls! Now his hair was nice and short, just the way he liked it. Today was his sister's birthday, but he was thinking about his own birthday–his ninth–which was coming up next month.

Sammie left his room, crossed the hall, and went into Daisy's room to give her the birthday card he'd made for her. When he didn't see her, he turned to place it on her dresser and noticed she had some coins sitting there. He leaned in and saw two quarters, three dimes, three nickels, and six pennies. Earlier, Sammie had asked his mom for some money for a candy bar at the store, but she told him she didn't have any change.

Daisy would be mad if she knew he had taken some of her money, but he'd tell her he borrowed it and would pay her back. He left the two quarters and took one dime, two nickels, and two pennies. He stuffed them into his pocket and ran downstairs.

Entering the kitchen, he said, "Hey Mom. Where's Daisy? I have a birthday card for her."

"Oh, that's so sweet of you, Sammie. I don't know where she is. She left with the boys quite a while ago. I'm actually starting to get a little worried. I need her home soon to get ready for her birthday party. Would you mind hopping on your bike and riding up to the playground to see if you can find her?"

"Awe, Mom! Do I *have* to?"

"Come on, Sammie, please? Could you do your mother this one favor? It would really help me out."

"Fine. I'll go."

"Thank you. Maybe later, I'll buy you a candy bar for your troubles."

"Okay! It's a deal," he said.

He ran out the back door and hopped on his bike.

"Try to hurry up, Sammie."

"I will!"

Sammie pedaled up the same street the three kids had ridden up only a few hours earlier. He headed for the school playground, taking the same shortcut that all the kids used. As he rode down the alley trying to ride around the potholes and large rocks, he spotted what he thought was Patrick's bike near an old garage. He slowed down to check it out.

Yep. That's Pat's bike.

He pulled over, got off his bike and put down the kickstand. As he rounded the corner of the garage, he saw Daisy's new bike and Michael's bike standing just outside the door of an old, rundown shed. He tiptoed to the shed and pulled on the door. It didn't open, so he used both hands and pulled harder. That worked and he peeked inside.

"Daisy? Are you in here?"

No answer.

He peered inside. The place was dark and dusty and had big cobwebs in the corners.

Creepy.

He opened the door a little wider and looked around. He saw some old tires and tools laying on the floor, and an old workbench off to the left. He was afraid the kids might sneak up and scare the wits out of him like they usually do.

"Daisy? Patrick? Come on you guys. I know you're in here. It's not funny. You're *not* scaring me. Mom's looking for you Daisy. You'd better come out."

More silence.

No one answered and no one jumped out to scare him.

"Hmm."

They must not be here, he thought. Where they are? Why would they leave their bikes sitting here? Someone could steal them. Daisy would be in big trouble if anything happened to her new bike. Maybe they were fooling around and went into that scary, haunted house. He hoped not. He did *not* want to go in there looking for them.

Instead of heading for the big, scary house, he stepped a little further into the shed. Turning to the right, just past the door, he saw something shiny reflecting off the thin ray of sunlight sneaking in through the cracks of the shed's wall. He walked toward it to see what it was and saw a dirty, old gumball machine that was tipped against the wall of the shed.

"Hmm. Strange."

He reached for the machine and tipped it upright. As he did this, he could see and hear all the hundreds of gumballs rolling into their new positions.

He wondered how old these gumballs were and whether gumballs expired. He couldn't help himself. He wanted a gumball and he didn't care how old it was.

He reached into his front pocket and took out the change he'd taken from Daisy's dresser. He checked the machine and saw that it needed nickels to work, so he kept the two nickels and returned the rest of the coins to his pocket.

He wondered what color he'd get. He wanted a purple one but then decided that his favorite color was green. He shrugged. Either would be fine. He liked to make his lips turn colors. That was the best part of gumballs. He loved to sneak up on his mom and scare her with a big roar and his scary purple (or green) lips.

Still feeling nervous about the scary shed he was in, Sammie quickly slipped a nickel into the slot and turned the crank. It creaked as he turned it, but soon, he saw an orange gumball start to make its way down.

He frowned. "Awe, man. Orange? Yuck!"

He watched it roll down and around and around.

Suddenly, from far away, he heard a strange sound. He wasn't sure, but it sounded like a scream. It sounded—tiny—and he had no idea where it was coming from. That's when the gumball machine started to shake.

13 The Shakedown

INSIDE THE GUMBALL MACHINE, and about five minutes after they started eating their gumball lunch, the Gumble house started to shake. Everyone ran for cover.

Daisy, Patrick, and Michael felt the entire gumball world move and vibrate. They got up from the table and ran to each other, losing their balance and banging into furniture as they tried to get to the front door. The thundering noise created by all the moving gumballs vibrated in Daisy's chest.

"Earthquake!" shouted Patrick.

Gordy put up his hands. "No. This is *not* an earthquake. This is a shakedown. You'd better go," he shouted. "This may be your only chance to get home. You need to run back to the spot where you arrived. The lid should open soon, but it won't stay open for long."

The children nodded and quickly said their goodbyes to Gordy and his family, and to Vinnie.

"Thank you for everything," said Daisy. "It was a fun and amazing experience that I will never forget."

They shook Gordy and Vinnie's hands as Gordy followed them out the door. He ran with them, shouting directions.

"Do you remember when we walked down Pink Street?"

"Yes! I remember," Michael said.

"Good. Just continue down this street—Yellow Street—until you get to Pink Street. When you get to Pink Street, take a left and go all the way down. Do you think you can find the place where you landed when you first got here?"

Michael nodded. "Yes. I think so."

"I sure hope so," Patrick said.

Daisy nodded. "I hope so, too."

"Okay," Gordy said. "You'll have to go back up and over the hill. That is where the lid is. I'd come with you, but it's too dangerous. You'd better hurry, or you might not make it before it closes again."

"Thanks, Gordy," Patrick said. "We'll miss you gumball guys!" He patted the large gumball on his smooth, round back, and then started jogging down the road with the other two kids.

Michael turned back to wave and saw Gordy's figure growing smaller in the distance. "Thank you, Gordy, and thank Vinnie and all the gumball people," he shouted. "It's been fun!"

Gordy waved. "Goodbye!"

The kids gave him one last wave and then turned and picked up speed, running as fast as they could down Yellow Street.

When they turned left onto Pink Street, they saw thousands of plain gumballs rolling, bouncing, and jumping all over the place. The kids had to zig-zag around and sometimes jump over the gumballs, but they continued to run at top speeds.

"It's like dodgeball at school," Patrick said.

Daisy pointed toward a hill up ahead. "*That's* not like dodge ball!"

They stopped and looked up. At the top of the hill, was a mass of plain gumballs rolling down toward them. This was the same hill they'd slid down just a few hours earlier, and it was the same hill they now needed to climb.

Daisy looked at the boys and yelled. "Where did they all come from? We'll never be able to climb the hill!"

Michael shook his head. "You're right! We're not going to make it!"

The floor of the gumball machine shifted beneath their feet, making them stumble and scream.

"Ahh!"

"It's no use," Michael shouted. "We *have* to go through them. Don't stop! Let's go!"

Michael started running again and Daisy and Patrick followed him. They jumped over and around the sea of gumballs and were nearing the bottom of the hill when they heard a thundering crash. They stopped and looked up. Thousands of gumballs were rushing down the hill and heading straight for them.

Patrick put his hands to his cheeks. "Ahh! Avalanche!"

"Keep going!" Michael yelled.

They continued toward the avalanche, running, jumping, and tripping over hundreds of gumballs that rolled around their ankles and shins. When the wall of gumballs was about halfway down the hill, Michael fell and was quickly pinned against a tree. Unaware that Michael was trapped, Daisy and Patrick kept running.

"Pat! Daisy! Help me—I'm stuck!" Michael screamed. "Don't leave me! You guys! H-e-l-p!"

Daisy and Patrick heard Michael's calls for help and stopped.

They turned and Daisy screamed. "Michael!"

She and Patrick ran toward him, pushing and kicking the gumballs out of their way until they reached him.

Patrick reached out to Michael. "Dude! Grab my hand!"

Michael stretched out his arm, but Patrick's hand wasn't close enough. There were still too many gumballs pinning him to the tree.

"Ahh! Come closer!"

Daisy looked back and saw the avalanche of gumballs closing in on them.

"Hurry Patrick!"

Patrick stretched his arm and body closer to Michael. "I'm trying!"

More gumballs filled in around Michael's ankles, making it harder for Patrick to reach him.

"Hurry!" he screamed.

Patrick kicked through the gumballs and stretched his arm a little closer. Finally, Michael was able to grab it. Daisy held onto Patrick's waist, making a short chain, and together, they pulled their weight backward. Slowly, Michael was pulled from his trap. He rolled on top of the sea of gumballs until he was finally able to stand on his own.

"Thanks, you guys! I knew you'd never leave me!"

Patrick raised his fist in the air. "Never!"

"Come on," Daisy said. "We need to hurry! Let's go!"

Her legs burned as they ran to the bottom of the hill and started their climb, but this was no time to rest. They had to hurry before the lid closed!

14 Going Home

AS THEY APPROACHED THE TOP OF THE HILL, Daisy remembered there was another small hill to run down. Going downhill was much easier, and she was glad there were no more gumballs in their way.

Looking ahead, Daisy pointed. "You guys—there it is! The lid! It's still open! I hope we're not too late!"

"Hurry!" said Michael.

The closer they moved toward the lid, the faster they ran. Their legs were tired and rubbery, but they knew they had to press on or they'd miss what might be their only chance to escape.

As they approached the lid, Daisy smiled and said, "I think we're going home!"

Michael did a little skip. "Come on—get in!"

The three of them jumped in the hole at the same time and immediately crashed into one another. They slid down the tunnel, screaming, but after falling only a short distance, they came to an abrupt stop, slamming tightly on top of each other.

"Ugh!"

"Ouch!"

"No!"

They hadn't fallen very far, and now they were stuck. Daisy was upside down with one of her arms pressed against her head. The pinch of the boys' bodies squishing hers, made it hard to breathe. She looked up past Patrick and Michael and saw the pink gumball sky through the opening just above them. She tried wiggling and squirming, but nothing happened.

To make matters worse, Patrick's stinky tennis shoes were right on her face.

Yuck!

Just above Patrick, was Michael, sitting directly on top of him.

Patrick shouted upward. "Hey! Get off me, Mike! You're heavy!"

Michael shouted down to him. "Sorry, dude. I can't. I'm stuck and my legs won't move."

"This is great," Daisy said. "What are we supposed to do now?"

15 Tennis Shoes!

IN THE HOT SHED, Sammie watched as the big gumball machine started to shake. He stumbled backward to get away from it, slamming his back against the shed wall. The shaking and rumbling machine jumped. That was enough for Sammie. He tripped and stumbled his way out of the shed and back to his bike. Rubbing his back and breathing hard, he looked down the alley hoping someone would come and help him. He turned to his left and then to his right.

No one.

The only sound he heard was the gumball machine shaking and banging inside the shed. He watched as the wall moved back and forth.

Bang! Bang! Bang!

Oh, boy. Not good!

He was about to take off on his bike when the banging noise stopped. The shed was quiet, the only sound coming from a singing robin that flew onto a tree branch just above him. Sammie tiptoed back to the shed's door and peeked in. The gumball machine was tipped and leaning on the back wall near a hole that wasn't there before. It was still vibrating and shaking a little.

What kind of crazy gumball machine is this?

As he walked toward it, a strange noise came from the top part, near the clear globe that held all the gumballs. This sound was different. It wasn't the shaking and rumbling noise like before. This sound was more like a cracking sound, and it got louder and louder.

Sammie put his hands to his head and smeared them down his face. He couldn't handle this.

"I'm out of here."

He turned and walked toward the shed's door and was just about to leave when he thought he heard someone scream. He stopped and turned back to look at the gumball machine.

That's weird.

The scream stopped and started again. It seemed to be coming from *inside* the gumball machine.

How could that be? It's impossible for a person to be inside a gumball machine. Impossible!

Maybe it was a *haunted* gumball machine, like the haunted house up the hill. He wanted to run, but his legs felt like cement and his feet wouldn't budge.

As he stared at the machine, he thought he saw movement near the top. He squeezed and blinked his eyes—hard—and leaned in. Sticking his neck out to get a closer look, he saw what looked like a tiny hand. A human hand! He blinked some more and shook his head, hoping to clear his vision. That didn't work because the little hand was still there.

Next to the hand, was a—a head? Yes. It definitely was an upside down head. The tiny hand and the tiny head moved slowly, like a slow-motion video.

The next thing Sammie saw made him straighten up. Near the upside down head and the hand, were two feet wearing tennis shoes and they were flopping and kicking like crazy.

"Hey! I've seen those tennis shoes before!"

16 Falling

INSIDE THE GUMBALL MACHINE, Daisy, Michael, and Patrick wiggled and squirmed as they tried to untangle themselves.

"How are we going to get out of this?" Patrick moaned. "We could die up here!"

"Don't say that Pat," Michael said. "That's *not* going to happen. We'll figure something out."

"It's *Patrick*. My name is *Patrick*, not *Pat*—and not *dude*!"

"Whatever, dude! This isn't the time to complain about what name I call you!"

"You guys! Stop arguing! Let's try to think!"

Daisy struggled to breathe, and yelling at the boys wasn't helping matters. Of the three of them, she was the most uncomfortable because she was upside down.

"Well, obviously we can't all fit down the slide at once," Patrick yelled from above. "That's why we're stuck. We have to somehow get free from each other and go down one at a time."

"Hey, I have an idea," Michael said. "We need to go down one at a time, right?"

"*Ah, yeah*. Isn't that what I just said?" Patrick asked.

Michael ignored Patrick's tone and continued. "So, the two top people—which would be Patrick and me ..."

"Duh," said Patrick.

Michael clenched his teeth and continued, "... we'll have to reach up and try to grab the opening and hang on."

"I don't know," said Patrick. "What if it shuts on our fingers?"

"Ah! Hurry up you guys! The blood is rushing to my head," cried Daisy. "Ugh. I don't feel very good."

"If the lid starts to shut, we'll have to let go," Michael continued.

"Okay," said Patrick. "Let's do it."

"Hurry!" Daisy moaned.

"Okay, okay! We're going!" Michael shouted. "Patrick—on the count of three—one ... two ..."

"Wait! Wait!" Patrick interrupted. "Is that one … two … three … and *then* jump? Or is it one … two … three–jump on three?"

Daisy moaned. "Ugh! I'm getting dizzy down here!"

"Okay, okay," said Michael. "Patrick, it's one … two … three … and *then* jump. You got it?"

"Got it," said Patrick.

"Okay. Ready?"

"I'm ready!"

"One … two … three … *jump!*"

Daisy cried out as both boys kicked away from her. They were finally untangled! She fell hard onto the slide–head first–and on her stomach. At the same time, Michael and Patrick reached over their heads and scrambled to grab the ledge of the gumball machine's floor.

Michael hung there, his feet dangling beneath him. "It worked!" He looked down at Daisy. "Oh, man! She's going down fast!"

"I've never heard her scream like that," Patrick said laughing.

Daisy heard her own screams ringing in her ears as she quickly swirled down, and around the slide.

"Ahh!"

The sucking force gripped her body. It felt as strong as it did on the ride up–and the air felt just as cold. Frost instantly caked onto her face, her hair, her hands, and her feet. An icicle formed on her hair and banged her cheek, stinging her skin, as she zoomed down and around the tunnel heading toward the bottom of the gumball machine.

Still dangling at the top of the slide, Michael said, "Okay, Patrick. Your turn. Go ahead. Let go. I'll come down right after you."

Patrick frowned. "Oh, Michael. I'm scared!"

"Dude! We have to hurry or we're going to lose some fingers!"

"Okay, okay. I'm going. See you at the bottom."

"Yep. See you at the bottom."

This reminded Patrick of the last time they said that to each other. It was at Pudding Hill.

Funny.

He realized at that moment, that if he could go down Pudding Hill, he could do this, too.

He was about to let go when the gumball machine started shaking and wobbling.

"Whoa! Michael! What's happening?"

The lid above their heads rattled and groaned as it tipped toward them.
"Go!" Michael shouted.

Patrick let go and fell–feet first–screaming all the way down.

"Ahh!"

The lid made a loud cracking noise and started falling forward. Michael let go. He heard Patrick screaming underneath him, but Michael's own screams quickly drowned out any other sounds. He whooshed and swirled down and around the slide screaming all the way, as frost built up on every part of his body.

"Ahh!"

17 No Way!

BACK IN THE SHED, Sammie watched as a tiny body whipped down the track inside the gumball machine. He thought he saw an arm, an upside down head—and—those *tennis shoes*. He definitely recognized those tennis shoes. At first, the arms, legs, and feet were tangled up, and because they were so small, he couldn't see them very well. Then, they untangled and someone started falling down the swirling slide toward the bottom. Then, he saw someone else fall—and then someone else!

When he looked closer, he couldn't believe his eyes. The faces looked just like his sister, Daisy, and her two buddies, Patrick and Michael!

"No way! How'd they get in there?"

18 Here They Come!

DAISY BOUNCED AND TURNED, the wind taking her breath away. As she neared the bottom of the slide, everything slowed down. At the final turn, her body started to shake.

"Uh-oh. Not again! H-i-c-c-u-p!"

She felt that same jolt shoot through her body, and that same sucking force pulling her forward. She couldn't wait to get *out* of this gumball machine.

"Ugh! Why do I have to be upside down for this?"

At the bottom of the tunnel and still on her stomach, Daisy banged her head as she came crashing through the opening

"Ouch!"

As soon as her body fell to the floor of the shed, she gurgled out a *huge* hiccup. Her body shook and jerked until she stretched back to her normal size.

She looked around and saw her brother, Sammie, sitting on his knees, staring at her, his mouth hanging open and his eyes wide.

"Daisy? Was that *you* in the gumball machine? How'd you get in there? How'd you get so small? What the heck is going on? Why are you all frosty?"

Daisy crawled over to him and gave him a big hug.

"S-S-Sammie, you—you s-s-saved us! I'm so happy to see you! Oh! You feel so nice and w-w-warm. This *shed* feels so nice and warm!"

She felt the frost on her face quickly melting, the water dripping down her cheeks.

"Daisy! What were you *doing* inside that gumball machine? How did you get in there?" asked Sammie. "And why do you have a big icicle on your head?"

"Ask me later, Sammie. Right now, we have to help Michael and Patrick. They're coming out right now!"

From inside the tunnel, they heard Patrick's screams. When they turned toward the gumball machine, they saw him swirling around, feet first and headed for the opening at the bottom of the tunnel. Daisy and Sammie heard his hiccups getting louder and louder.

Daisy was still out of breath and slightly dizzy from the wild ride (and from being upside down for so long) when she turned to Sammie.

"Quick! Sammie! Help me get them out!"

They crawled back to the opening of the gumball machine, ready for the first body to come flying through.

"Seriously, Daisy. What were you guys doing in this gumball machine?"

"I told you, Sammie. I'll tell you later. Now, help me get the guys out. Look! Here comes Patrick!"

They watched as Patrick slid around and down.

"He's much louder than you were," Sammie said.

"A-a-h! H-i-c-c-u-p! H-i-c-c-u-p!"

Daisy yelled up the tunnel. "Don't hiccup too soon, Patrick!"

"Like I can—h-i-c-c-u-p—help that!" he shouted.

As Patrick landed near the bottom, he stopped just before the opening. Daisy pounded her fists on the outside of the slide.

"Get out, Patrick! Hurry! Michael is coming right behind you! I can see him!"

Patrick's feet were now out of the machine, but he was having a hard time pulling out the rest of his body. He turned his head to look up and saw Michael coming straight for him. Michael's screams were getting louder and he was getting closer.

Patrick turned to Daisy. "Get me out of here! Hurry! Michael's coming! He's going to flatten me!"

"That's what I just told you!"

"Pull my leg! Pull my leg!"

He was just inside the opening and Daisy saw the scared look in his eyes.

"I'm trying! I'm trying!" She grabbed one of his ankles and leaned back. "Come on, Sammie! Help me!"

Sammie knelt next to Daisy and grabbed Patrick's other foot. "I *knew* I'd seen those tennis shoes before!"

"Keep pulling!"

Sammie yanked and pulled on Patrick's foot. "He's really stuck!"

"Oh no!" She said. "He's too big! He hiccupped too soon, and he's stretching back to his normal size!"

"I think he's stuck!" Sammie said. "He looks so weird—like a snowman!"

They heard Michael's voice coming from above Patrick's head.

"Get out of the way! I'm c-c-coming!"

It was too late. Michael's feet slammed into Patrick's shoulders.

"Ooh-owie!"

Patrick shot out of the slot, landing on top of Daisy and Sammie.

"Owe!"

"Ugh!"

"Ooh-owie-e-e!"

The three of them moaned as they tried to untangle themselves.

At the same time, Michael hiccupped and shook, but, unlike Patrick, he easily slipped out of the machine. He crawled onto his hands and knees, and the others watched as his frozen body shook and jerked. He jerked so hard, he fell back against the shed's side wall, nearly breaking through it.

Patrick and Daisy ran to help him up, but they didn't have the strength. Instead, they fell down around him. They giggled and hugged each other as Sammie stood over them and watched.

"We d-d-did it!" Patrick said. "We're b-b-back to our normal size!"

They stayed on their hands and knees, shivering and breathing and melting and laughing. Sammie sat down beside them, waiting for someone to tell him what had just happened.

The four kids sat on the floor of the dusty shed for several minutes, catching their breath.

"Seriously, you guys," Patrick said. "Was all of that j-j-just a dream?"

"You guys look so cold," said Sammie.

"You have n-n-no idea," replied Michael. "It feels s-s-so nice and t-t-toasty in here."

Patrick nodded and rubbed his sore shoulders. "We m-m-made it, you g-g-guys! We're h-h-home!"

"Oh b-b-boy, I have never b-b-been so happy to be any place in my life. I love this old shed," Daisy said.

She smiled and high-fived Patrick and Michael.

"I can't believe we actually made it back alive," said Patrick.

They turned and looked at Sammie, who had stood up and was now staring at them, his mouth hanging open.

"Do you guys have any idea how *cool* that was? How did you do that? I want to try! Can I try?"

The three of them put out their hands, shook their heads, and shouted, "No!"

"Well, I put my nickel in there. I wanted a purple gumball or a green one, and the only thing that came down the shoot was an ugly old orange one—and then *you* guys came down after that. *Somebody* owes me a gumball!" Sammie folded his arms and frowned.

"I'm telling you, you do *not* want the green one," Daisy said, still remembering Steeler's cold, mean face.

Daisy, Patrick, and Michael looked at each other and then back at Sammie. He was the one who put his nickel in the gumball machine, causing the big shakedown. They owed him big-time for saving them, so they high-fived him, hugged him, rubbed his head, and thanked him several times. They also promised to get him as many gumballs as he wanted—only *not* from this machine.

With frost melting from their faces, and water dripping onto their shirts, they realized just how grateful they were for Sammie's help. They were also grateful for the knowledge of how to get back home if this should ever happen again though they doubted it would. Even though they had met some cool gumball people, and had had some fun, they never wanted to go near that gumball machine again.

19 Daisy Makes a Decision

AS THE FOUR OF THEM WALKED into Daisy and Sammie's kitchen, their big brother, Joe, walked in from the living room.

"What's the matter with you guys? You look like you've seen a ghost, or something," he said, laughing and shaking his head. "What a bunch of losers."

Ignoring the "losers" comment, Daisy began telling Joe about their adventure. "We got sucked up into this gumball machine we found over in the old shed by the playground, and we were up in this beautiful gumball world with real gumball people!"

Joe leaned back and laughed. "*Gumball* world? *Gumball* people? What are you talking about?"

"It's true!" Patrick said, as Michael nodded.

Joe frowned and shook his head. "Either you guys have completely lost your minds, or you're lying to me because you're doing something you're not supposed to be doing. I'm *definitely* telling Mom and Dad that you guys are up to no good."

He turned to leave the room.

"*Gumball* world. *Gumball* people. Yeah right. And I'm Superman! Now I've heard everything."

He chuckled as he climbed the stairs.

Michael turned to Daisy and Patrick. "You guys—he thinks we're lying!"

"Who cares?" Daisy said. "What does he know?" She looked around. "Hey—what time is it?"

Patrick looked at his watch. "What do you know? It still works! It's three o'clock."

"My party! It's almost time!"

"What time does it start?" asked Michael.

"Four o'clock. I have to go. Sammie, tell Mom I'll be right back."

"Where are you going? Mom wants you here," Sammie said.

"I'm going over to the new girl's house, right now, to invite her to my party."

"But what about what Joe said?" asked Michael.

"Who cares what Joe said? We just learned what it's like to be the new kid, didn't we? Remember how uncomfortable we felt when we first came into the gumball world?"

The boys nodded.

"She's right," Patrick said. "The gumball people were looking at us like we were aliens, or something. I don't know about you guys, but I was really scared."

Daisy nodded. "And remember that horrible green *Steeler* gumball guy? He was so mean! That was horrible. I've never been so afraid or felt so terrible in my *whole* life. Worst of all, he didn't even care about my feelings. He just kept saying terrible things about the way I looked. I hated that. I hated that he was looking at me as if he was better than me. I'm not used to anyone looking at me like I'm different, and, for the rest of my life, I will never make anyone feel like that."

The boys nodded and gave her a small smile.

Daisy pointed at the boys and smiled. "And—remember how nice most of the gumballs were to us? It didn't matter to them what we looked like or that we were different. That was nice and that's how it's supposed to be."

"You're right," Patrick said.

Michael nodded. "Yep."

"So," Daisy said, "how do you think Violet would feel if we treated her like Steeler treated me? She doesn't even have a different *shape* than we do. We all have a *human* shape. So what's the problem?"

"No problem," Michael said. "We need to do what's right."

Patrick nodded. "Yep. That stuff never mattered to the gumballs."

Daisy threw up her hands. "That's what I'm trying to say. If the gumballs can do it, then so can we."

"Yeah," Patrick said. "Like—for example, our skin is soft and the gumballs' is hard." He nodded and smiled.

"Ooh! I have one," Sammie interrupted. "Their skin tastes good and ours doesn't. Right Daisy?"

Daisy chuckled. "That's right."

The boys laughed out loud.

"How about this one?" Patrick said. "We have hair, they don't. We have skin, they don't. We have legs, they don't."

"Exactly," Daisy said. "The gumballs showed us how to treat each other."

Michael nodded. "We can't listen to people like Joe. If we did, we'd probably miss out on meeting some really nice friends."

"And gumballs," added Patrick.

"Okay," said Daisy. "I still have time to run over to Violet's house, introduce myself, and invite her to my birthday party. I can't believe I listened to Joe. Why would I do that?"

"Because he's really good at making you believe what he says," Sammie said.

"You're right," Daisy said. "He's *very* good at it."

"You'd better get going," Michael said.

"I hope I'm not too late."

Daisy ran to the back door, down the steps, and around the side of her house until she reached the front. She paused, looking across the street.

I hope she's home.

She looked both ways before she walked across the street. Once on the other side, she started to run. As she approached the door, it opened before she could even knock. It was Violet. She was wearing a pair of blue shorts, and a yellow t-shirt. Her long, black hair was pulled back into a ponytail.

Breathing hard, Daisy smiled. "Hi. You're Violet, aren't you?"

"Yes, I am. You must be Daisy. My mom told me that you live across the street. I saw you earlier this morning riding your bike with two boys. It's nice to meet you."

"It's nice to meet you too. Those boys are my friends, Patrick and Michael. I'll introduce you to them."

Violet smiled. "That would be great."

Still breathing hard, Daisy said, "I hope I'm not too late, but I would like to invite you to my birthday party. It's this afternoon."

"This afternoon?"

"Yes. I know it's kind of last-minute. It starts at four o'clock. I really hope you can come. My mom said you will be going to our school. You will like it. The kids are really nice."

"It would be very nice to meet some of your friends. Oh—but if your party is in an hour, I don't think we'll have enough time to get you a present," said Violet.

"I don't care about a present. I really want you to come. Do you think you can ask your mom?"

"Wait here. I'll go ask."

Violet turned and walked down the hall, shouting up the stairs. "Mom! Daisy from across the street is here. Can I go to her birthday party? It's today!"

While Violet was away, Daisy smiled.

A new friend.

A moment later, Violet returned to the front door with her mom.

"Hi Daisy, I'm Violet's mom, Mrs. Hanson. It's very nice to meet you."

Mrs. Hanson was tall and thin with short, dark hair. Daisy liked her warm smile. She was wearing jeans and a t-shirt and she looked like she had been busy unpacking.

"It's very nice to meet you, too, Mrs. Hanson," Daisy said. "I'm sorry my invitation is so late, but can Violet come to my party today?"

"If it's okay with your parents, it's okay with me," replied Mrs. Hanson.

"I already asked them. They said it would be great if she could come."

"That's wonderful!"

Turning to Violet, Mrs. Hanson said, "Sweetheart, you'd better go upstairs and get ready. You have a party to go to!"

Violet smiled and turned to Daisy. "What should I wear?"

For the first time, Violet took a good look at Daisy. Following Violet's gaze, Daisy looked down at herself. She was filthy. It looked like she hadn't brushed her hair in a week. It was sticking out all over the place. She was still a little bit wet and sticky from Pudding Hill—and—there was dirt from the shed stuck on top of that.

Daisy rubbed her face and looked at the ground. "Sorry. I had a rough morning. That's why I look so messy and why it took me so long to come over and invite you to my party. Don't worry though. I don't *always* look like this. I mean, I won't be wearing this to my party, of course," she laughed. Violet laughed too.

Violet's mother smiled and said, "Don't worry about it. I'll let you two decide what to wear to the party. I have to get back to my unpacking. It was nice to meet you, Daisy."

"It was nice to meet you, too," Daisy said.

Violet's mom walked down the hall and turned the corner.

"What happened to you? How did you get so dirty?" Violet asked.

Daisy grinned and leaned in toward Violet. Whispering she said, "It's a long story. I'll tell you later. You aren't going to believe it."

"Okay," Violet said, giggling.

"Oh," Daisy said. "I'll be wearing a short-sleeved blouse and a flowered skirt. I love flowers."

"So do I," smiled Violet. "I'll wear something with flowers, too."

Daisy smiled as she thought about how Patrick and Michael would hate to be a part of this girlie conversation. Finally, she had the girlfriend she had dreamed about. She knew they would be good friends.

Daisy said goodbye to Violet, crossed the street, and ran up the stairs and into the front of the house.

"Mom! Dad!"

She couldn't wait to tell them the news. Her parents came out of the kitchen and into the living room. They stopped short when they saw Daisy's messy appearance.

Daisy's mom put her hands to her face. "Oh my gosh, Daisy! What happened to you? You're a mess! Did you go swimming or something? What happened to your hair? And what's this pink gooey stuff on the back of your shirt?"

Her dad frowned, as he picked off some of the dried pink pudding from Daisy's shirt. "It looks like bubblegum or something."

Daisy didn't know what to say. "Um, no, I didn't go swimming, exactly. The guys and I had a little adventure this morning."

"Oh boy. Not another adventure, Daisy. I don't even want to know what you did to get that gum on the back of your shirt, young lady. That will *never* come out. We'll probably have to throw it away. And your hair—it looks like you were in a windstorm or something! Is that *gum* in your hair, too? Ugh! This is what happens when you play with boys. They love to get messy!"

There was no way Daisy could tell them that she really *was* in a windstorm, or that she flew up into a gumball machine. They'd never believe her. She would try to tell them later. All she could say for now was, "Sorry about that, Mom."

"Honestly, Daisy. I don't know how you'll have enough time to get your hair washed and dried in time for the party. I'm not sure that gum will *ever* come out of your hair. We may have to cut it out."

Her dad interrupted. "Well, we'll talk about this mess and where you've been, *after* your party. For now, you'd better hurry up. Your guests will be arriving soon, and your mom and I have lots to do to get the food ready."

They turned to leave. "Wait," Daisy said. "I almost forgot to tell you. Guess what? Violet—the new girl from across the street—is coming to my party!"

"You invited her? I didn't even introduce you yet," said her mom.

"I went over and introduced myself," Daisy said smiling.

"Well, good for you! That's a very grown-up thing to do," said her mom.

"I thought you were afraid to ask her to your party," said Daisy's dad.

"I know. I was afraid before, but I figured some things out and marched right over there. I'm not sure why I was so afraid. That was silly. She's really nice."

"That's terrific!" said her dad. "Now, go upstairs and get ready." Turning to Daisy's mom, he said, "Honey, will you help me in the kitchen?"

Daisy's mom and dad headed back to the kitchen. "Get up there, Daisy."

"Okay!"

Daisy ran up the stairs to get ready for her party.

20 Daisy's Birthday Party

IT WAS FOUR O'CLOCK and Daisy was finally ready for her party.

She was upstairs when she heard the doorbell ring. "Right on time," she said.

She took one last look in the mirror. Her hair was down. It looked nice and wavy—and pretty. Her mom would be happy to see that all the gum (pudding) came out. Her yellow blouse and flowered skirt looked much better than the dirty clothes she had on earlier.

She took one last look in the mirror.

Much better!

She ran downstairs and answered the door. It was Patrick, Michael—and Violet. All three had presents in their arms.

"Happy birthday Daisy!" they all shouted together, laughing.

"Oh, thank you! Look at all of those presents! Thank you so much!" said Daisy. "I see you guys met Violet."

"Yep. We met her as she crossed the street," said Michael.

"Well, come on in. The party's in the backyard."

They walked through the kitchen where Joe was picking at the cake. Daisy slapped his hand.

"Get out of my cake!"

"Oh. I see all of your *friends* are here. I heard no one else could make it," Joe said. He gave them a nasty grin.

Daisy was embarrassed by her brother's comment. She hoped Violet didn't notice what he was trying to say.

"Go ahead, you guys. I'll be right out," Daisy said.

After the door shut behind her friends, Daisy turned to Joe and said, "Can you be any more rude?"

"What?"

"I'm telling Mom you're being mean."

Joe shrugged his shoulders and smiled. "Go ahead, see if I care."

The doorbell rang and Daisy shoved her brother into the counter as she left the kitchen to answer the door. Three more of her friends from school—Katie, Rebecca, and Amanda—had all arrived carrying gifts. They wished her a happy birthday and started chatting and laughing.

Daisy led them through to the backyard and introduced them to Violet. After everyone had arrived, Daisy counted fourteen guests. She never realized how many friends she had, and it made her feel happy.

After the party had gone on for a while, Daisy was finally able to sit down with Violet for a moment to talk.

"I like your name," said Violet.

"Thanks. I like your name, too," said Daisy. "Hey, that's why we like flowers so much, isn't it? Both of us are named after flowers!"

"Yep and they're pretty flowers, too," added Violet.

"There sure are lots of pretty colors in the worlds," Daisy said, thoughtfully.

"You mean world. There's only one world."

"Huh? What did I say?"

"You said, 'worlds' with an 's' on the end—like there is more than one world."

"Oh. Right. I meant 'world'." Daisy giggled. "Whoops!"

"Well, anyway, you're right. There sure are a lot of pretty colors in the world," Violet said.

Daisy had a good feeling that she would finally have a girlfriend. She couldn't wait to start their friendship.

"Hey Violet, remember when I said I'd tell you how I got so dirty and messy today?"

"Yes," Violet said.

"Well, this is what happened, but don't tell the other kids, okay? It'll be our little secret."

"Okay," Violet said smiling.

Daisy started her story from the beginning, at the old shed, and told her everything that happened to her and the boys. Throughout her story, Violet would interrupt her and say, "No way. That can't be true."

Daisy would nod her head and say, "I know it's hard to believe, but it is true. Just ask Patrick and Michael. They'll tell you."

Daisy continued with her story and told her everything up to the part when she arrived at Violet's house a little while ago.

"Wow. That is an amazing story. I still can't believe it's true," Violet said. "It seems like a fantasy."

"I know. I feel the same way," Daisy said. "If I didn't have so much trouble pulling the dried pink pudding from my hair, I would have thought it was a dream, too."

Patrick and Michael joined the two girls. "What's happening you two?" Patrick asked.

"I just told Violet about our adventure today."

Michael smiled at Violet. "Pretty amazing, huh? I keep thinking it might have been a dream, but it wasn't."

Violet nodded. "It sure *sounds* like a dream, although it explains why Daisy looked like such a mess a couple of hours ago. It really is an amazing story. I wish I could have been there with you guys."

They continued their conversation until it was time for cake and ice cream.

The party was a huge success. They talked, danced (Patrick did his robot dance again) and played games. Later, Daisy opened her presents.

Later, Violet came and sat next to Daisy. "This is a great party, Daisy. Thanks for inviting me. Your friends are really nice."

"You're welcome. I'm glad you could come and I'm glad you were able to meet my friends. I knew you'd like them."

As they walked toward the food table, they saw Michael pull something from his pocket.

"Hey. Where'd these gumballs come from?" he asked Patrick. Patrick looked into Michael's hand.

"Maybe they came from 'you-know-where,'" Patrick said, laughing. "Maybe they'll start hiccupping and turn into gigantic gumballs right before our eyes and then roll over all of us."

Patrick started laughing so hard, he had to hold his stomach.

"That's not funny, Patrick," said Michael.

Peering down at the palm of his hand, both he and Patrick stared at the gumballs, and then blinked and looked closer.

"What the heck?"

Patrick reached for one of the gumballs and, as he did, it moved in Michael's hand. He jumped and yanked his hand back.

"Whoa!"

Some of the party guests stopped talking and looked over at them. Michael put up his hands as he spoke to them.

"Don't worry. Everything is fine. It's nothing. Never mind." He gave them a weak smile and a quiet giggle. "Go back to what you were doing."

The two boys turned their attention back to Michael's hand.

Michael held it closer to their eyes so they could be sure they were seeing what they *thought* they were seeing.

"Hi Michael!" said the two smiling gumballs as they waved their little hands.

"Remember us? Gordy Gumble and Vinnie Gumba? As you can see, we have a bit of a problem and we need your help. We were sucked back with you and ended up in Michael's pocket right before the lid closed."

"Uh-oh," was all Michael could say.

Coming up from behind them, Violet asked, "What's the matter?"

Michael squished his hand together and brought it behind his back. He could hear Vinnie and Gordy mumbling something. Violet frowned and tried to look behind him. Michael pulled his hand back in front of him and opened it to show her.

She threw her hands to her cheeks. "No way!"

Patrick tried to stay calm. "Violet, could you get Daisy, please?"

"Be right back."

Violet took off running and returned with Daisy.

"What's up?" Daisy asked.

"It's more like—what's down," said Michael as he uncurled his fingers.

The four kids stared at the two little gumballs in Michael's hand.

"Uh-oh," Daisy said.

"You guys were telling the truth, weren't you? Look at those cute little talking gumballs," Violet said.

The two gumballs smiled and waved. "Hi, Daisy!"

Daisy ran her hands through her hair as she looked at the boys. She started talking super-fast. "What the heck are they doing here? How are we going to get them back? We can't let anyone see them—or hear them."

The boys shook their heads. They had no answers to Daisy's questions.

Daisy's voice got very quiet. "You guys, we're in *big* trouble!"

Hi!

Do you want to find out what happens next? Check out the sequel:

Life in the Gumball Machine – Vinnie and Gordy's Return

Turn the page to read a sample!

Life In The Gumball Machine – Vinnie And Gordy's Return
Maureen Bartone

Turning the cup sideways, Michael carefully rolled the little gumball guys into it. Vinnie and Gordy felt themselves tip and spin. They banged into each other as they rolled to their new temporary home.

Michael looked down at them and said, "Will you guys be okay in there?"

The two gumballs looked at him and gave him their thumbs-up.

"Okay, let's get you into the house."

He covered the cup with his hand. Daisy and Violet ran with him in through the back door of Daisy's house just as the thunder started clapping, and the rain began pelting their heads.

Once inside, the party seemed even louder. Everyone was excited as they laughed and talked about the surprise thunderstorm. Daisy's mom and dad were asking her guests to call their parents and let them know the party was over.

Michael placed the cup containing their surprise visitors on the coffee table in Daisy's living room. He kept a close eye on it, making sure the loud group of kids standing nearby wouldn't bump the table.

After a few minutes, he became distracted with all of the excitement and chatter. When he peeked in on Vinnie and Gordy, they were still in there and doing fine. He then took a moment to call his mom to let her know he was staying at Daisy's a bit longer. He finished his call just as the other kids raced to the window to look at the lightening show going on outside. He too, ran to the window to watch the excitement.

Meanwhile, Daisy's dad was walking around the room with a garbage bag, tossing the discarded plastic cups and plates.

Michael's heart skipped a beat as he remembered his precious cargo. He turned to the coffee table to pick up the cup containing Vinnie and Gordy, but when he saw that the cup was no longer on the table, he threw back his head and groaned. Daisy heard him, and came running.

"What's wrong?"

She followed his gaze as he watched her dad heading into the kitchen with a large, black garbage bag. Daisy couldn't believe her eyes and grabbed Michael's arm.

With a sharp whisper she said, "I thought you were watching the cup!"

Michael whispered back. "Yell at me later. Let's go—before they get thrown into the dumpster!"

The thought of that made them look at each other and then dash toward her dad. They caught up to him just as he entered the kitchen, and then slowed down before he saw them.

Daisy's dad was popular with all of her friends. He was tall and thin with short brown hair, and his brown eyes were warm and kind. He was funny and friendly, and he was always willing to help any of them out any time they needed it.

Daisy appreciated the hard work her parents did for her party, and always wanted to do her part. But this time, she had an ulterior motive.

"Here, Dad. Let me help you." She took the bag from him.

Her dad smiled as he released it to her. "Why thank you, Daisy. That's very nice of you. Just leave it by the back door. I'll take it out to the dumpster after it stops raining."

"Okay," she said.

He left her to handle the bag, and went to the sink to start washing dishes. She turned to Michael. "Help me with this, will you? It's kind of heavy."

"Here, give it to me," he said.

He dragged it to the kitchen door. With her dad still in the kitchen, all they could do was leave the bag, and look at each other. Michael widened his eyes and jerked his head toward her dad. He mouthed the words "*now what?*" Daisy shrugged.

They had no choice but to return to the living room, leaving Vinnie and Gordy somewhere down in the dark and nasty garbage bag.

Once back in the living room, they lingered near the swinging kitchen door, occasionally peeking in the kitchen to keep an eye on the garbage bag.

Michael leaned in and whispered to Daisy. "How will we *ever* find them in all of that disgusting trash? Yuck!"

"Easy," Daisy whispered back. "We'll just call to them. Their voices will guide us."

Michael smiled and nodded. "Excellent point."

Patrick and Violet noticed Daisy and Michael acting strangely near the kitchen door.

"I wonder what they're doing," Patrick said.

"Let's check it out," Violet said.

Some of the children had already been picked up by their parents, and the rest were still in the living room laughing, talking loudly, and acting silly. Daisy's mom was saying goodbye to one of the guests when she called to Daisy.

"Daisy, please come and thank your guests."

"Be right there Mom," she called. Turning to Michael she said, "Don't take your eyes off of that bag."

When Patrick and Violet walked over to them, she told Michael to take turns with them, so it wouldn't look suspicious.

"I don't know what you're talking about, but it *already* looks suspicious," Patrick said.

"Yeah," Violet said. "What's going on?"

Michael explained what had happened, and that Gordy and Vinnie were now slogging around in the ice-cream-and-cake-trash.

Patrick wrinkled his face. "Yuck!" he said. "That's disgusting!"

Just thinking about their two little gumball pals swimming in the sweet and sticky garbage made him shiver.

"I know," Michael said. "We need to get them out of there—soon! They're not supposed to get wet."

When the last of Daisy's guests left, Daisy's mom asked Patrick and Michael if they needed a ride home.

"Pretty soon, Mrs. Lannon," Michael replied.

She walked past them and went into the kitchen, the door swinging behind her. Daisy stopped at the kitchen door with the rest of them.

"Is everything still okay?"

"Yep. Your dad's still in there cleaning," Michael said.

"What's the plan?" Violet asked.

"We wait, I guess," Michael responded.

"Wait for what? No way. We need to get in there now or it will look too obvious," Patrick said.

"He's right," Daisy said. "We need to go in there and act natural. Violet and Patrick, you sit at the table next to the bag, and Michael, you and I will start helping them clean."

Michael agreed. "Good plan. Ready?"

The others nodded and headed into the kitchen. Daisy went to the kitchen sink where her mom was washing dishes, and started to help her dry the larger bowls and pans. Her mom thanked her with a smile. The two of them had done this hundreds of times, so it seemed natural to her mom, even though Daisy's stomach felt like it was filled with butterflies.

Michael grabbed the broom and started to sweep the kitchen floor, while Patrick and Violet sat at the table near the garbage bag containing their new friends, Vinnie and Gordy.

Daisy's dad left for a minute, and returned to the kitchen with another garbage bag. He set it on the floor and stuffed more party trash into it. As everyone worked, Patrick and Violet heard some miniature-sounding shouts coming from the garbage bag, and Patrick jumped from his seat.

"Whoa!" he yelled. Michael, Daisy, and her parents stopped and looked at them. Violet hadn't moved, but her eyes were wide and her mouth hung open.

"What's wrong?" asked Daisy's dad as he approached Patrick and Violet.

"Sorry. It's nothing," Violet said. "We just saw a big bug and it crawled right by Patrick's foot. It was pretty big and it just startled us. We're fine." Violet smiled and tried to act casual. She hoped Vinnie and Gordy kept quiet.

Daisy's dad asked where the bug went, and started searching around the garbage bag near Violet's feet. Because he was so close to it, all four children started talking at once, trying to distract him—hoping he'd move away from it.

Daisy's dad frowned and stared at them. "What is *wrong* with you kids?"

He turned, reached down and grabbed the garbage bag. Violet and Patrick jumped up from their seats, but said nothing. Mr. Lannon picked up the second bag with the same hand, opened the back door with his other hand, and before the kids could do anything, he tossed them both out the back door and clear across the back porch. The bags banged into one another as they landed near the edge of the stairs.

INSIDE THE GARBAGE BAG, Gordy and Vinnie flew up and around.

"A-a-h-h! Gordy! What is happening?" Vinnie shouted.

"Hang on Vinnie! It'll be over soon!" Gordy shouted.

Gordy clung to a dirty paper cup and crawled in just as they landed and bounced across the porch.

Boom! Boom! Ka-bang! Bop!

The bag landed hard and then stopped. Still in the paper cup, Gordy banged and rolled around in it a couple of times before stopping. Putting his hands to his mouth, he shouted out to Vinnie.

"Are you okay Vinnie?"

Vinnie was able to plant himself in a piece of leftover cake and frosting. He got smacked by some paper cups and plates, but the cake cushioned his landing.

"I think so!"

They sat inside the bag—quiet and still—and worried. This world was a dangerous place! They heard muffled voices, and felt more movement. Gordy felt himself roll back and forth inside his cup.

"Uh-oh. Here we g-o-o again!"

Vinnie plunged both hands into the cake and frosting and grabbed on. He didn't want to be tossed around again.

Inside the paper cup, it was impossible for Gordy to brace himself because there was nothing for him to hold onto.

For an instant, the garbage bag Vinnie and Gordy were in leaned on the other bag until its weight pushed them both tumbling down the five steps, rolling over and over.

"A-a-h-h!"

The bag landed in the wet grass with a hard thud. Deep inside, the stinky, hot garbage flipped and flopped, sending Gordy and Vinnie deeper into the trash. The two tiny gumballs could hear the pouring rain spatting onto the plastic bag as they scrambled to get themselves upright.

Tic-tic-tic-tic. Tic-tic-tic-tic.

IN THE KITCHEN, the children stared out the door, their mouths open. Violet held her hands to her cheeks. They knew Vinnie and Gordy were no longer in the safety of the paper cup. They'd failed miserably in keeping the little guys safe, and it hadn't even been an hour. At this rate, they'd never make it through the night.

From the kitchen sink where she was doing dishes, Daisy's mom looked over at the kids. She frowned and shook her head.

"What is *wrong* with you kids tonight? You sure are acting strange. It's just a small thunderstorm. Honest to goodness, you'd think you saw a ghost or something. I think it's time for everyone to go home. It's been a long day."

Daisy's dad agreed. "Come on kids, I'll drive you home."

Patrick turned to look at Daisy's dad. "But … "

He was worried about Vinnie and Gordy out in the storm. The rain continued to pour, and the dark sky was lit only by the occasional flash of lightening. He was also terrified of the thunder but didn't want to admit it. Everyone knew thunder was nowhere near as dangerous as lightening, but still, it made him shake. Though he tried to hide it, he was afraid to go out in the storm to rescue them.

"But what?" asked Mr. Lannon.

Daisy had to think fast. Walking over to her mom she said, "Can't they stay a little longer? I don't want my birthday party to end yet." She clasped her hands together and used her best puppy-dog eyes.

"*Pl-e-e-a-s-e?*"

Michael, Patrick, and Violet each gave Daisy's mom a similar pleading look.

Mr. Lannon turned to his wife and smiled. "I don't mind if they stay. But it's up to you."

Daisy could see it in her mom's face. She was caving. Mrs. Lannon tried to frown, but underneath it was the slight curve of a smile.

She sighed. "Okay. Your friends can stay one more hour." She looked at Michael, Patrick, and Violet. "But call your parents and let them know."

"Yay!" The four kids celebrated with high-fives all around.

Daisy's dad shook his head and smiled. His wife sure was a softy. When it came to the kids, she always had trouble saying no. She smiled back at him.

Trying to sound stern, he said, "Fine. One hour. Not a minute longer. Got it?"

The kids nodded, trying to hide their relief.

After the phone calls were made and Daisy's parents went upstairs, the kids sat around the kitchen table to plan their next move.

"Man, that was close," Michael said.

Violet nodded. "It sure was. *Now* what do we do? It's still pouring."

Michael sat back in his chair and looked up, as if the answer was on the ceiling. He put his finger to his chin and tapped it. The others waited and watched him think. After a moment, and with a smile and a glimmer in his eye, he sat up.

"Okay. Here's the plan. Three of us will go out there and dig through the trash, while one of us keeps a lookout for Daisy's parents."

Patrick raised his hand. "Ooh! Can I be the lookout?" he asked.

Violet was new to the group, so she had no idea that Patrick was a scaredy-cat. But Michael and Daisy knew. When they were stuck up in the gumball machine earlier this morning, he was terrified to explore the strange little world. He was also the last one to jump over the cliff onto Pudding Hill because he was so afraid.

Oh, yes, they knew. And now, his shaking foot told them everything. He did *not* want to go out in that storm. So, when Patrick asked if he could be the lookout, there was just no point in arguing.

"Sure Patrick. You can be the lookout," Michael said.

Relieved, Patrick slumped. "Thanks."

With Patrick now on guard-duty, Michael gave Daisy and Violet their assignments.

"Daisy, do you have an umbrella?"

Daisy nodded and walked to the broom closet near the kitchen sink. She opened the door, reached in and pulled out a long, black umbrella. As she walked back to the table, Michael continued giving his instructions.

"Okay. Daisy, you hold the umbrella."

Turning to Violet, he said, "Violet, you hold open the garbage bag while I dig through the trash."

Michael's body shivered a bit, as he turned down his lips and scrunched his nose. The thought of digging through that pile of sticky, dirty, smelly trash grossed him out. The girls gave him a funny look.

"Are you going to be able to do this?" Violet asked.

Michael took a breath. "Well, as usual, no one else is going to do it, so I *have* to."

"Hey, it's your fault they're in there in the first place," Patrick said.

Michael raised his hands in front of him. "I know. I know."

He wanted to kick himself. The thought of being up to his elbows in garbage, made his stomach turn. But it *was* his fault, so he accepted the job. He turned to the group.

"Okay. Is everybody ready?"

Daisy's eyes widened. "Wait! I have an idea."

The other three watched as she walked to the kitchen sink, bent down and opened the cupboard underneath. When she returned, she held a pair of rubber gloves.

"Here. My mom uses these to clean the dishes. They protect her fancy nail polish."

Michael smiled. "Thanks. This will definitely help."

He put the gloves on, and then raised his hands out near his waist. "Okay. *Now* is everybody ready?"

"Wait! I have another idea," Daisy said. The other kids chuckled as she went back to the broom closet and found a flashlight. Returning to the group, she handed it to Michael.

"You'll need this, too."

Michael nodded. "Yes I will. Good thinking."

He then grabbed an apple from a bowl sitting on the counter and handed it to Patrick. "If someone comes into the kitchen, take a big bite of this apple and chew it while you're answering any questions they may ask you. They won't understand a word you say."

Taking the apple, Patrick smiled and nodded. "Okay." He sniffed it. "Mmm. I love apples."

Michael looked out the window near the kitchen table and said, "The thunder and lightning stopped, so it should be safe to go outside."

Michael turned to Daisy and Violet. "Ready?" The girls nodded.

He opened the door and the three of them stepped out onto the back porch. Although the worst of the storm had passed, it was still pouring rain, and it was getting dark. Daisy opened the umbrella.

After Michael shut the door behind him, Patrick could hear the girls' squeals as they ran down the porch stairs and into the rain. He sat at the kitchen table holding his apple. The room was silent, but not for long. He took a huge bite of the juicy red fruit.

Crunch!

Chewing loudly, he waited, still feeling a bit nervous and anxious. He wondered how Vinnie and Gordy were doing.

———————————

Thanks for reading the sample! I hope you enjoyed it. You can find the book online at many of the top retail locations. Search:

Life in the Gumball Machine – Vinnie and Gordy's Return

Thanks for reading *Life In The Gumball Machine.* I hope you enjoyed it! I appreciate your feedback. While it's fresh on your mind, I hope you'll write a review and let me know what you think!

~ Maureen Bartone ~

Other books by Maureen Bartone:

Life in the Gumball Machine – Vinnie and Gordy's Return

Tilly's Top-Secret Trapdoor
National Indie Excellence Awards® FINALIST

ABOUT THE AUTHOR

Maureen Bartone is a National Indie Excellence Awards® FINALIST. She lives in the Twin Cities, Minnesota, with her husband, Geno. Together, they have three children, and two grandsons. Her favorite things are family, music, writing, dancing, and laughing, but especially being a wife, mother, and grandmother.

Would you like to know when Maureen's next book is available? You can sign up for her new release e-mail list at www.MaureenBartoneAuthor.com. You can also follow her on twitter at @BartoneMaureen, or like her Facebook page at https://www.facebook.com/MaureenBartoneAuthor.

Follow Maureen Bartone on Social Media!

https://www.facebook.com/MaureenBartoneAuthor

https://www.linkedin.com/pub/maureen-bartone/53/49/258

http://www.goodreads.com/author/show/6518759._Maureen_Bartone

https://twitter.com/bartonemaureen

https://www.pinterest.com/maureenbartone

https://plus.google.com/101057748350459045841/posts